Buried Secrets

By

Cheryl Kennedy

Argus Enterprises International, Inc
New Jersey***North Carolina

Buried Secrets © *2012* All rights
reserved by Cheryl Kennedy

A-Argus Better Book Publishers, LLC

For information:
A-Argus Better Book Publishers, LLC
9001 Ridge Hill Street
Kernersville, North Carolina 27285
www.a-argusbooks.com

ISBN: 978-0-6156138-6-4
ISBN: 0-6156138-6-1

Book Cover designed by Dubya

Printed in the United States of America

1978

Turning off the main street onto the rough gravel road leading to the summer cottage, Philip glanced again in his rearview mirror. Knowing she would follow him, he had loosened the bulb of one headlight enough that it would flicker on and off like a beckon, making it easy to recognize her vehicle even in the complete darkness of the back roads. As he rounded the corner he turned off his own headlights before steering his car off the road and parking it just behind the tall sea grass separating the road from the beach beyond. Smiling to himself as he watched her pass him, he lit a cigarette and settled in.

He had waited too many years for this moment, all the while suffering through countless social functions with her and her highbrow Newport friends. Never had they welcomed him into their circle, always looking at him with something between pity and amusement. He had been nothing more to her than a way to get back at her father; a game with no winner and he was the pawn.

Glancing at his watch, he snuffed out the remainder of his cigarette and opened his car door. By now, he was certain, she had checked the cottage and was searching for him on the beach, hoping to catch him in the act for yet another opportunity to ridicule him. He shook his head recalling the countless times she had used his middle-class upbringing as a means by which to make herself feel superior.

It was he who had suggested they buy the property that had long been abandoned by its previous owners. All his research had led him here and he was certain that given the opportunity he would soon locate some of the missing treasure from one of the of shipwrecks history recorded on the Rhode Island coast. Taking the direction of the currents and the last known position of the various ships into consideration, the cove was the most logical resting place for the cargo as well as whatever remained of at least one large vessel, if not more.

It was only because of her mother's drunken ramblings one night when the others had gone to bed that he had even become aware of the vast treasure thought to be buried just below the surface of the sandy beach surrounding the cove. Angered by the hours she had spent alone while her husband studied the charts and delved into the history of the ships lost on the Rhode Island coast, she had turned to the bottle for comfort.

His jaw tightened as he recalled how Katherine had laughed at him despite the many years of research and hard work that had brought him here. She had agreed to purchase the property only because of its proximity to her precious Newport, but found his theories an embarrassment and insisted that he not discuss them in front of her circle of friends.

Now, as he was closing in on the location of what he expected to be a vast fortune, she had decided that she was no longer interested in indulging his fantasies and had advised him of her intent to sign the property over to her sister Sarah, a free-spirit who preferred the simpler things in life, a notion that boggled the minds of Katherine and the rest of her family.

Stepping onto the beach, Philip scanned the shore, spotting his wife perched on the rocks overlooking the ocean. As he moved in her direction, the sound of his heart pounding in his ears drowned out the crashing waves. Her back was turned to him as he climbed up the slippery rocks and approached her.

Without turning, she spoke.

"What game is it we're playing tonight, Philip?" She asked before turning to face him.

"No game, Katherine, I merely decided to come out one last time to say goodbye."

Philip stood firm, looking past Katherine at the ocean rather than in her eyes as she insisted he do when addressing her.

"I'm over here, Philip; look at me when you speak to me." She demanded, crossing her arms across her chest and drawing back her shoulders in superiority.

"I'm tired, Katherine," he said, glancing at her before again looking off in the distance.

"Tired of what exactly? You speak in riddles; spit it out of God's sake. Be a man for once."

Philip turned, approaching her so quickly that she backed away, clinging to the edge of the slippery rocks with her manicured nails.

"Tired of you, Katherine; tired of your superior attitude, your friends, who by the way only call themselves that to associate with your father and his money. I'm tired of having to beg for what you should gladly give and of being a puppet to your every whim. I may not come from money like you did, but I'm not a stupid man. I won't have you toy with me any longer just so you can amuse yourself. You know how important my work is to me and yet you take everything I've worked toward and you give it away, simply because you can."

"How dare you speak to me this way?" Katherine shouted over the crashing waves. "Don't think for a minute there won't be repercussions for your words, Philip." Though she stood her ground her eyes frantically searched behind her at the rock's edge that was becoming dangerously close.

"I will speak to you however I wish, Katherine, I'm done with these games." At that he moved two steps forward forcing her backwards to the edge of the rocks.

"Goodbye, Katherine." He said, smiling as he took another step forward causing her to step back and lose her footing. As he stood motionless, he watched as terror filled her eyes and she fell backward, slamming her head against the cold wet rocks before slipping under the water.

Chapter 1

As the darkness of her unconscious mind faded away revealing slivers of light, Emily slowly awoke. Before she opened her eyes, accepting that she was no longer asleep, her arm stretched across the bed, her fingers spread wide, searching for the man that should be lying next to her. Moving her hand back and forth across the cool sheets, she held her breath, slowly opening her eyes to confirm what she already knew.

It had been nearly two years since her fiancé Chase had died, yet still each morning she found herself searching for him, hoping that perhaps she was finally waking from a long, painful nightmare. It was only then when her mind was still foggy from sleep that she thought it was possible that it had all been a dream. Though the days had turned to months and the months to years, the pain was as raw as it had been the morning following the accident.

Brushing away the single tear that escaped her eye and ran down her cheek, Emily swallowed back the lump in her throat that threatened to choke her. Frustrated by her inability to get past this painful morning ritual she sighed; pulling back the covers and rolling out of bed.

The curtains billowed as the warm summer breeze filled her bedroom with the salty air of her coastal retreat. Pulling back the sheer white curtains to reveal a perfect blue sky, Emily breathed deeply, closing her eyes and allowing her senses to carry her away to happier times.

The cottage had originally been owned by Chase's Aunt Sarah and had been the setting for some of his fondest childhood memories. Never married, Sarah was

Chase's mother's sister. His mother, Katherine, had died when he was only seven years old, leaving him alone with a father who preferred his solitude to spending time with his son, who was more often than not, simply an annoyance and an inconvenience to him. Luckily for Chase, his Aunt Sarah cherished the time he spent with her and so, when he wasn't away at boarding school; he spent his time at the cottage where she filled their time with all kinds of adventures.

Emily smiled recalling the stories Chase had told her about his adventures searching for buried treasure on the beach, digging for clams and fishing off the dock. Aunt Sarah wasn't uptight like his father, who Chase couldn't recall wearing anything other than a three-piece suit. Shoes, she told him, were for sissies. They spent their summers barefoot, the dirtier the better. Chase was twelve before he realized his aunt would slip out at night to bury small treasures in the sand for them to find the next day. He had never let on that he knew; after all, half the fun was her excitement when he uncovered a rusty pocket watch or a bottle with a love note in it. They would spend hours, their feet dangling off the dock into the salty ocean, as they puzzled over who might have left the treasure behind and whether someday the person would return to the shore in search of their long lost item.

It was the imagination she had awakened in him that had led him to become a writer. When she died, Sarah had left the cottage to Chase, along with all the memories they had shared. That was five years ago and yet, as Emily looked around the room that had been Sarah's bedroom, it was as though she was still there. Though they had never met, Emily felt as though she had known Sarah her entire life. Walking over to the dresser, Emily picked up a small seashell from a collection within a bowl made of driftwood and fishing net. Emily smiled; recalling how Chase had described how he and his aunt would walk the beach every morning, collecting whatever they thought was interesting in a Nantucket basket. When they could find nothing else, they would return to the cottage and spread out their treasures on an old quilt. All morning long, while they lazily fished at the dock, they would debate what they should make with the items they had found. She recalled how he had told to her with great pride how he had taken the driftwood and netting from the quilt one day while his aunt was busy preparing lunch and hidden them under his bed. Later that night while his aunt was drinking her evening tea on the porch, Chase had glued together the various pieces of driftwood in a circular shape and strung the netting in the middle. He had hidden the bowl for weeks until her birthday, collecting tiny shells each day to place inside it. When the morning of Sarah's birthday finally arrived, Chase had proudly presented her with the homemade gift. Chase had beamed as he described how she cried like a baby, hugging him until he was certain there was no air left in his lungs.

Emily sighed, wishing she had been a part of their adventures. Theirs was a bond that would never be broken. Even in death, the memories of their past were all around her. No wonder Chase never wanted to come back here after she died. It didn't make sense at the time. She recalled his stubborn insistence that he wouldn't return to this place, when his aunt had first passed. Emily had tried to reason with him. His aunt wanted him to have the little cottage, situated on the shores of Jamestown. His aunt obviously wanted him to stay connected to their past and all that they had shared during the many summers they spent here. And yet, Chase had refused, insisting that he wanted to remember those days through the eyes of a young boy and not as a grieving adult.

As the years had passed, Emily had tried several times without success to change his mind. Finally, a couple of months before his own untimely death, Chase had agreed that it would be nice to spend the summer weekends away from their tiny apartment in Providence and had begun to spend his Sundays driving out to the cottage to get it ready for the summer. It was on his way home from the cottage that Sunday night two years ago that Chase had driven off the road and into the cold ocean waters where he met his death.

When she had awoken that morning to find Chase already gone, she had stretched lazily feeling the cool sheets between her fingers. Wrapping her arm around his pillow she had closed her eyes and breathed deeply, the faint smell of his cologne still clinging to the pillowcase, lulling her back to sleep. When she finally crawled out of bed, it was mid morning and the sun was high in the sky. She had considered driving out to Jamestown to surprise him, but a flat tire had derailed the plan and she had spent the day reading his latest work.

Chase had called her around dinnertime to tell her he had lost track of time and that she should eat without him. He assured her he wouldn't stay much longer. After eating dinner alone, Emily had settled on the sofa to watch TV and had eventually fallen asleep while waiting up for him.

It wasn't until she woke to the doorbell ringing and someone pounding on the door that she realized something was wrong. Half asleep she had staggered to the front door and opened it to find the local police standing solemnly before her. What they said to her was still a blur to this day, which was probably for the best. She recalled feeling faint and being asked if there was anyone they could call to come and be with her.

Later, Emily had been stunned to find out that he had willed the property to her, assuming that it would be returned to what remained of the family, and had resisted the urge to come, knowing that it would reopen still sensitive wounds. But when her career had taken a different path, leading her to open a small bookstore on Newport's Thames Street shopping district, she realized that commuting from Providence every day was out of the question. It just made sense to move to Jamestown when her landlord had sold the apartment building and the new owner was giving the tenants options to stay under their current rental agreements or leave without penalty. And so, with her furniture placed in storage and the last of her boxes packed into the back of her car, she had crossed the Jamestown Bridge to the cottage and her new life.

Chapter 2

While he continued to pace back and forth in front of his large office window overlooking the Newport harbor, Philip unconsciously tugged at the stiff collar that was ever threatening to choke him to death. How many years had he been forced to play the role of the grieving widower, been shackled to his father-in-law's business as a means, not only to survive; but to keep tabs on the land that was rightfully his?

Settling back down into his black leather executive chair, he looked around him in bitter contempt. The furniture reeked of old money, from the intricately carved mahogany desk to the hide-away bar complete with Waterford crystal decanters and the finest liquor money could buy.

Not one item in the office belonged to him and yet he was forced to rot here along with any hope he had of returning to his true passion.

Turning his chair to face the ocean, he sadly reflected on his youth. The carefree days of a young man piloting fishing vessels for the wealthy tourists while putting himself through college; he had been just twenty-one when he met Katherine. Her father had commissioned the boat for a weekend trip to Martha's Vineyard. Accompanied by his wife, daughter and a potential investor, he had paid extra for Philip to not only pilot the vessel, but to serve as a steward as well.

Katherine's obvious attraction and flirtatious behavior toward Philip had not gone unnoticed by her parents and the more they scolded her, the more outrageous her conduct became. Even all these years later, when he held nothing but hatred in his heart for her, he had to smile at her ability to undermine her parent's authority. She had made it her mission that weekend to capture the heart of Philip, a game solely played to enrage her Father who had refused to rent her a loft on Providence's East Side where she attended Brown University; instead insisting that she live at home where he could better keep an eye on her.

Positioning herself on the deck of the boat in full view of Philip, she had started the game by removing her bikini top and lying on her back to sun herself while her Father and his client were fishing off the back of the boat. As usual, her mother was below deck, avoiding both the sun and the company of her husband while she drank her boredom away. While Philip had enjoyed the view, he wasn't stupid enough to risk the large tip he was sure to get by acknowledging her advances.

When her father had finally seen her, he had demanded she join her mother down below. Katherine, however, was not to be so easily dismissed and had waited until her father was deep in conversation with his client before returning to the deck and requesting that Philip rub sun block on her back. By the time the sun had set and her parents were entertaining their guest on the island, Katherine had managed to convince Philip to join her for a swim.

One thing had led to another and by the end of the weekend he had been hooked and her Father, thinking he could buy his way out of the embarrassing situation had agreed to rent her the apartment on the condition she end her relationship with Philip.

"Oh, but you were never one to back down, were you, Katherine?" He said, looking at her photo which remained prominently placed on his desk to remind him every day of the life she had taken from him.

Absently picking up an antique brass hand compass from his desk, Philip once again spun around to face the ocean, watching as the needle twisted in response. After

Katherine's death he had no choice but to back off, allowing her sister Sarah to take possession of the cottage as well as the property surrounding it. His opposition to Katherine's wishes would have only aroused questions that were best not pondered. As far as her family was concerned, the property had only been purchased as a charming summer retreat to entertain, not because Philip had considered it to be the resting place to a fortune in buried treasure.

When Sarah had suggested that his son Chase spend summer vacations with her at the cottage Philip had agreed, hoping that when Sarah either passed on or tired of the place she would sign the deed over to his son and Philip would once again be able to resume his search of the land. Unfortunately, it had taken over 25 years for that to happen forcing him to endure the suffocating life of a businessman. Tugging again at his overly starched collar he longed for the past when he wore t-shirts and shorts and his biggest concern was the daily marine forecast.

His secretary's voice on the intercom interrupted his reverie.

"Mr. Bohman? Mr. Sinclair has arrived. Shall I show him in?"

Philip glanced at the clock, grimacing at the thought of having to suffer through another meeting with the pompous investor. As the vice-president of Excursion Charters, it was Philip's job to acquire potential lucrative clients. His ability to charm even the toughest of clients had not gone unnoticed by his father-in-law and after years of proving his worth through his knowledge of just about everything relating to the sea and the marine industry, he had finally been given a position that paralleled his talents.

Turning around, he straightened his tie and pressed the intercom button.

"Yes, Kelly, show him in."

Stepping out from behind his desk just as Kelly opened the door, Philip strolled over to his client and extending his hand in greeting.

"Greg, it's great to see you. Come… sit down. Can I get you something to drink?"

An hour later, after sealing a deal with Greg Sinclair for a prominent showcase at the 2011 Newport Boat Show as the "Exclusive Excursion Charter Company" recommended by the Newport Tourism Council, Philip shock his hand once again and showed him out before returning to his office.

As he sipped bourbon it was far too early to drink, he flipped through the morning paper, scanning the headlines but not really reading the articles. Picking up the business section of the paper his eyes fell upon the photo of a familiar face standing outside a downtown business. The caption under the picture read:

Emily Gaudet, owner of Chase Your Imagination Books

That's why he recognized her; she had been his son's fiancé. Though he had been good to Chase, he had never had a strong bond with the boy. Katherine had been the doting parent. After she had died he had found it difficult to raise the boy on his own, opting instead to place him in boarding school rather than have him underfoot. He would arrange for him to come home for holidays and he would indulge him with expensive gifts and trips, but he never had any deep feelings for his son who was the spitting image of his mother.

Sarah had provided Chase with the parental guidance and affection he lacked and for that he was grateful. Though he resented the fact that she considered

Chase more a part of her family than Philip would ever be, he felt secure in the knowledge that his patience would eventually pay off.

Chapter 3

Swallowing the last bite of toast and washing it down with her now cold coffee, Emily surveyed the tiny kitchen. There was barely enough room to navigate between the boxes that were stacked precariously between the kitchen table and the counter. Shaking her head, she admitted to herself that she should have taken things a bit more slowly in regards to moving in.

Rather than continue the long commute, she had begun moving boxes in only a month ago. Each morning she would fill her car with as many boxes as she could fit then, after work, she would drive to Jamestown and drop them off at the cottage before returning home for the night. On the weekend evenings she would move furniture to the storage unit she had rented with the help of friends she would bribe with pizza and beer.

After moving the last of her things in over the weekend she now sighed realizing that she probably should have unpacked the boxes as she was dropping them off. The cottage was small enough without being filled with boxes.

"Oh well" she said, setting her dirty plate and cup into the sink, "you live and you learn."

After brushing her teeth and dragging a comb through her long, dark hair she maneuvered through the maze of boxes to the front door. Turning around once again to scan the mountains of belongings she would have to face when she returned home from work she shook her head in defeat.

Driving the short distance from the cottage to her little bookstore, Emily made a mental list of what she needed to pick up on her way home. She hadn't gone grocery shopping in weeks, knowing that whatever she bought she would have to move. Living on fast food and the occasional evenings out with friends, she had grown accustomed to shopping at the various convenience stores along her commute. A loaf of bread here, a gallon of milk there; not only was it an expensive way to shop, it was getting really old after doing it for a month. She missed cooking, although it had lost some of its joy now that she was cooking for one, but still, she found it therapeutic in a weird sort of way.

As she pulled off of Thames Street into the little alley adjacent to her shop, she parked her car and reached into the backseat for her bag. Mondays tended to be the slowest day for business' the weekend tourists now gone and the locals still avoiding the busy shopping district where the bumper-to-bumper traffic of summer tourists annoyed even the most seasoned residents. Though she had only opened *Chase Your Imagination Books* six months ago, she was familiar with the pattern, being a life-long Rhode Island resident. Growing up in the area, Emily had starting spending her summers working in Newport at the age of sixteen. She had done everything from passing out menus to potential patrons along Bowen's Wharf to selling t-shirts and souvenirs for various shops on America's Cup Avenue. She smiled now, recalling the many summer romances she had as a young girl. Though many of the same faces worked the strip each summer, there were always a few new faces and Emily had found it hard to resist the bronzed boys with their gold-streaked hair.

As she turned her key in the lock at the side entrance to the shop, she could already hear the phone ringing. She dropped her bag just inside the door as she rushed to the tiny office in the back of the building. Of course, as soon as she reached it, the answering machine had picked up the call and she waited for the outgoing message to finish before she heard the dial tone indicating the caller had hung up.

"It's going to be one of those days," she said to herself before turning to go back to the door to retrieve her bag. Working seven days a week for the last six months was starting to take its toll on her and she was determined this week especially, given the fact she had a lot of unpacking to do, it was time to get some help.

Ideally, Emily envisioned herself running the little shop on her own, but she hadn't really taken into account that besides from stocking the shelves and tending to the customers, she also needed to handle the behind the scene duties including balancing the books and selecting and purchasing the books themselves. Her love of the "American Classics" had resulted in her decision to offer her patrons both new and used books, which had delayed the opening of the shop by more than a year. It was important to Emily that she be selective in her choices in order to set herself apart from the other bookstores in the area.

During the summer months of the previous year she had frequented yard sales and well as estate sales, collecting treasures their owners found of little or no value. Often times she would purchase an entire lot, later picking through the batch for the one or two books that were worth holding onto. The remainder of the books she would bring to used bookstores and trade them for store credit to purchase others she had not yet found.

It still amazed her that in this Internet age people were so naïve when it came to the value of their things. Shaking her head even now, she recalled the day she happened upon a yard sale that had not been advertised in the local paper. She had passed by it on her way to another sale and, seeing the owners about to shut it down on her way back, she decided to make a quick stop.

There were three large boxes filled with books, most of them paperback "Harlequin Romances" and she asked the woman how much she wanted for the whole lot of them. The woman had shrugged her shoulders indicating she really didn't consider them of any real value and was thrilled when Emily presented her with a ten-dollar bill. So pleased was she with the last minute sale, she offered up her husband to assist Emily in carrying the boxes to her car. Later that evening when Emily was sorting through the boxes, she was stunned to find a first edition copy of *Walden* by Thoreau. After researching its value and finding it worth more than five thousand dollars, Emily felt so guilty that she had anonymously mailed the woman a bank check for one thousand dollars.

During the winter months Emily had spent her weekends browsing through local consignment shops as well as buying books on the Internet. By the end of the year she had collected more than a thousand books and had decided it was time to open up the shop. The new books she carried were those written by Rhode Island authors, books pertaining to Rhode Island as well as a section specifically dedicated to her late fiancé.

The section of the shop dedicated to Chase was situated in the front of the shop and was introduced by a wooden sign hanging from the ceiling, which read, *Chase's Corner.* Two upholstered wingback chairs gave patrons a place to sit and read. A round mahogany table separated the chairs and provided additional lighting by way of a large lamp. In front of the chairs was a coffee table, which held one copy of each of the half dozen books he had published before he died. Behind the chairs stood a mahogany bookcase dedicated to multiple copies of each book. Next to the bookcase hanging from the wall was Emily's favorite picture of Chase, taken by his Aunt Sarah when he was a boy. In the photo he was wearing nothing but a pair of swim trunks, his feet dangling in the water as he fished off the dock. It was obvious that he had been unaware that she was taking the picture as he faced away from the camera, but despite the fact that only the side of his face was visible, anyone looking at the photo could see how happy and content he was.

The rapping at the shop door startled Emily, making her jump and she cursed herself for getting wrapped up in memories instead of getting to the business at hand. Acknowledging the mailman with a wave she headed to the front door of the shop to let him in.

"Sorry, Bill," She said grabbing the bundle of mail he had tucked under his arm so that he could set down the large box. "I was spacing out. I hope I didn't leave you standing there too long."

"No worries, I'm just glad you're in and I didn't have to walk back to the truck with this." He said, nodding toward the box. "The guy that usually delivers the big stuff is on vacation this week so they doubled my load."

Brushing the sweat from his forehead, he glanced around the shop. "I keep telling my wife we should come in here on one of my days off. It looks like you have some interesting stuff."

"That would be nice; I would be happy to give you a discount if you find something you like."

She smiled, hoping she didn't sound as distracted as she felt. The long hours were really getting to her and she often found her mind wandering these days. Even when she wasn't in the shop her mind raced with all the things she had to do. Picking up on her frazzled state, Bill bade her goodbye and left her to her duties.

By lunch Emily had cataloged the new books that had arrived, placed them on the shelves and dusted and vacuumed the shop. She still had to balance the books from the previous week's sales and pay the invoices, however the lack of food in her stomach made it difficult to concentrate and she decided a hearty lunch would give her the energy she needed to make it through the remainder of the day. Posting a note on the door that stated she was closed and would be back at 1:00, she locked the door and headed for the office to grab her bag. As she exited through the side door she again heard the phone in the office ring.

"That figures." She muttered to herself before continuing on her way. "Whoever it is can wait until I get back."

Chapter 4

As he continued to stare at the photograph of Emily in the newspaper, Philip drummed his fingers on the arms of his chair. First his wife, then her sister and finally his own son had stood in the way of his fortune while he had been forced to live his life relying on others to provide him with the lifestyle he deserved. Now, only two short years after he had resumed his work and was finally seeing results for his patience and determination, this woman had moved into the cottage and forced him to retreat once again.

Now, as he took a deep breath, he made his decision. His patience had finally run out. No longer could he sit in this stuffy office wearing the uncomfortable three-piece suits his father-in-law insisted he wear. No longer could he sit back and wait for his opportunity to take control of his life. He had suffered long and hard as a part of this miserable façade and grown more and more bitter as the months and years had passed. No, he resolved, he wasn't about to wait any longer.

Chapter 5

Riley stepped out of the smoky, dark pub into the mid-afternoon summer heat. Squinting his bloodshot eyes while he attempted to adjust them to the glaring sunlight, he reached in his pocket for his cigarettes and lighter. The private club was one of only a handful of establishments in the state that still allowed smoking, but Riley preferred to smoke outside. As he lit the cigarette and stuffed the rest of the pack back in his pocket his cell phone rang.

"Damn it!" He mumbled under his breath, "Can't a guy have a smoke in peace?" Pulling his phone from the back pocket of his dirty jeans he barked into the phone.

"What?" He demanded without bothering to say hello. It was too hot and he was too tired for any formalities.

"It's me." The voice said on the other end of the call. "Can we meet later?"

"Where?" Riley asked, certain he knew the answer.

"The pub in Portsmouth, seven o'clock."

"I'll be there." Riley said before ending the call, tossing the rest of his cigarette to the ground and heading back into the club.

As he downed the last swallow of the cheap draft beer, Riley tossed a dollar in the tip jar before making his way out to the parking lot and the cab the bartender had called for him. After doing six months in corrections for drunk driving several years ago, he had learned his lesson. It was either give up the booze or give up driving. His choice had been an easy one to make. He could live without a car, but he couldn't survive his miserable life without a few drinks under his belt.

"Where to?" the cabbie asked without looking back at his passenger. They were all the same to him, they all reeked of stale beer and smoke and none of them were considerate enough to tip him.

Riley mumbled the name of the pub in Portsmouth before leaning his head back and stretching out his legs. It was only a ten-minute drive but he could use a little shuteye. Working third shift on the docks, gutting and cleaning fish for a living was a far cry from what he had envisioned his life to be, but it paid for the sparsely furnished studio apartment he shared with a buddy from his past, as well as providing him enough drinking money to make it from paycheck to paycheck. He only needed a place to crash and shower, other than that he wasn't there long enough to consider it home.

"Hey Buddy, we're here." The driver announced, waking Riley from his short nap. "That'll be twelve bucks."

Riley reached into the front pocket of his jeans and pulled out a ten and a five dollar bill, still damp from sitting on the bar soaking up beer and condensation. "Keep the change." He said, handing the bills to the cabbie before crawling out of the cab.

"Hey, thanks, you have a good evening." The cabbie called out before Riley shut the door. Shaking his head as he watched him stagger toward the pub. "Just what you need, more booze." He said to himself before driving away.

Inside the pub, Riley scanned the crowd looking for the guy he knew only by face. Even though he had worked for him off and on for nearly three decades, the guy had never told him his name, which was fine with him. The less he knew the better. After all, it wasn't like their relationship was based on friendship; it was strictly a business partnership. As he approached the booth in the back of the room, Riley noticed that *the man* seemed slightly more agitated than usual. *Great*, he thought, *I wonder what he wants now*.

Sitting opposite *the man*, Riley motioned for the waitress and ordered a beer. The two sat in silence until she returned with the drink and then moved on to another table to take their order.

"So." Riley said, sipping the cold beverage and leaning back in the booth. "What's the job?"

The man looked around making sure that their conversation wasn't being monitored before leaning in to speak. "I need you to proceed with the plan we discussed. I can't take anything for chance this time; too many lives have been lost already. We need to step it up."

Riley considered the request. "How much?" He asked. There was no point beating around the bush when the stakes were high.

"Ten thousand" *The man* replied without flinching.

"Make it twenty and you got yourself a deal." Riley counter offered; it wasn't like the guy had any other options so he might as well go for double.

The man stared into Riley's eyes as if considering the offer. "Five up front, the rest when the job is done." He said, holding out his hand to shake on the deal.

Riley looked at it briefly without accepting the gesture, instead tossing back the rest of his beer before rising. "I'm gonna need a lift home." He stated, waiting for the man to oblige.

The hint of disgust briefly passed *the man's* face before he nodded, rising from the booth and leading the way out of the pub to the parking lot.

Chapter 6

After returning to the shop following a substantial meal, Emily was eager to get as much accomplished as she could in the remaining hours of the day. Checking her messages she found she had missed a call from one of her suppliers and spent the next half hour tracking down the list she had made the previous week of the books she had intended to order.

Next she contacted the local newspaper to place an ad for a part-time cashier that could assist her and take some of the pressure off as well as a full-time employee with experience in the retail business that could take over two days a week so she could take some time off, at least for the busy tourist season. Relieved at having accomplished at least those tasks while assisting the handful of customers that had stopped in, Emily settled in to go over the past weeks receipts.

She had just started going through the receipts when her phone rang.

"Good afternoon, Chase Your Imagination Books, this is Emily." She rattled off.

"Emily, this is Philip Bohman…Chase's Father." He paused allowing her to reply.

"Mr. Bohman … I must say, this is very unexpected." She responded, wondering why after all the years that she and Chase had been together and years after he had passed, he would contact her now.

"I apologize for not contacting you sooner, but like you. I'm sure, I was quite devastated over the loss of my son." Again he paused before continuing, "I thought perhaps you and I could get together for dinner."

"I appreciate the invite, Mr. Bohman, maybe in a couple of weeks. I could give you a call. I recently moved and my schedule is quite full right now between the shop and unpacking. I'm sure you understand."

There was a lengthy pause and Emily was about to ask if he was still on the line when he spoke.

"Yes... of course... I understand. I'll give you a ring in a couple of weeks and we'll make arrangements then. Goodbye, Emily." He disconnected the call before she had a chance to respond, leaving her wondering what had just happened.

When Emily and Chase had first starting dating she was eager to meet his family. Though she was aware his mother had died when he was very young, the stories he told of his summers at the cottage with his Aunt Sarah were like something out of a Mark Twain novel. Emily had been thrilled when Chase had suggested they spend the summer vacationing in Jamestown with his aunt. Unfortunately, Sarah had died two weeks before they were scheduled to arrive and though she had spoken to Sarah several times on the phone making arrangements for their visit, she never had the opportunity to meet her in person.

Chase's father had been another matter entirely. Though he held no animosity toward his father, he had never really developed any true feelings for him either. Chase recognized that his father had been unprepared to raise a son on his own when his mother had suddenly died and therefore understood his decision to send him to boarding school. He actually had been grateful for the fact that his father sympathized with his need to develop family bonds and had allowed him to spend his summer vacations at the cottage.

Staring at the papers in front of her, Emily realized the distraction of the call had derailed any likelihood that she would complete the task at hand and decided she had accomplished enough for one day. If she left now, she could avoid the rush hour traffic on the Newport and Jamestown Bridges and would still have enough hours left in the day to start unpacking some of the many boxes that awaited her at home.

As she drove in the direction of the cottage her mind drifted back to her relationship with Chase. She was just entering her senior year at Brown where she was working toward her Bachelor's Degree in business. Though she had already completed her core requirements for English she had been trying to get into the popular American Literature class for the past two years. Everyone she knew had raved about the handsome professor and author Chase Bohman and his unorthodox method of teaching. As a senior, she was finally able to obtain priority placement and was excited to meet the legend on campus.

Early into the semester she had set herself apart from the class through her eager participation and enthusiasm with the assignments. Her knowledge of American Literature had gained her recognition and she had soon found herself staying after class for private discussions with the professor. Though he was ten years her senior, their mutual appreciation of literature; especially that of the early American classics had quickly developed into a friendship that spilled out of the classroom and into social settings.

Emily smiled, thinking about the first time they had met for coffee at a little café on Wickenden Street in Providence. Though it was not against policy for professors to mingle with their students; it was highly frowned upon. Because theirs was a relationship based on friendship and not a romantic involvement, neither of them gave it much thought. Emily still recalled seeing him as she entered the café and realizing, not for the first time how incredibly attractive he was. She had found herself unable to follow the conversation as her mind had wandered and he had asked her with concern if everything was all right. Emily had felt the flush of her cheeks as she struggled to make up excuses for her distraction. Chase had told her months later that he had known exactly what the problem was because he too had struggled that day to stay focused.

The next time they had gotten together Chase had suggested they attend a poetry reading at a little hole in the wall outside of Providence. At the last minute he had proposed that they have dinner at a popular Italian restaurant on Federal Hill before heading to the reading. They had never made it to the reading, if in fact there was a reading. Months later Emily had asked him about that but he had only smiled and winked.

As she was pulling off the main street onto the gravel road leading to the cottage she realized she had been so wrapped up in her memories of the past that she had forgotten to stop at the grocery store as she had planned. Glancing at the clock on her dashboard she decided it was still early enough to change out of her work clothes, do some unpacking and still have time to get to the store before it got too late.

Stepping into the small living room Emily silently vowed to attempt to complete at least one room before taking a break and so, rather than change her clothes as she planned, she simply rolled up the sleeves of her button-down blouse and got to work. Luckily, she had at least been smart enough to label the boxes with their contents and she was able to quickly move more than half of them to the rooms they belonged in. Having cleared a space large enough to work in, Emily now got down to business, beginning with a box marked "books". Dragging the box across the room toward the built-in bookshelves she made quick work of piling the books on the bare shelves. She would organize them later once the room was completely unpacked, but for now she would just get them on the shelf.

As the summer sun slowing faded, Emily opened the last box, realizing for the first time that she had been on such a roll that she had neglected to stop for dinner. Apparently the big meal she had at lunch time had sustained her longer than she expected, as even now; though she was incredibly thirsty, she had no desire to eat. Making quick work of the remaining box and discarding it with the other, now empty ones; she plopped down on the sofa to admire her work.

While the work was nowhere near done, having accomplished so much in one night gave her hope that by week's end she would finally be able to move freely throughout the cottage without having to pick her way through mounds of boxes. Scanning the room, Emily acknowledged that the majority of the contents belonged to Sarah, who it appeared had similar taste to her own. From the casual off-white sofa littered with an array of pillows with a seaside theme to the repurposed lobster traps topped with thick pieces of glass for use as a coffee table and two side tables, the room fulfilled its promise of a relaxed retreat. The sheer window treatments allowed the salty air to flow through the room, inviting its inhabitants to indulge in all that the property had to offer. A pair of worn wicker chairs faced the sofa and separated the tiny dinning area from the rest of the room. The hardwood floors had seen better days yet added to the charm of the cottage, telling a story of the past with some areas more bare than others. Small pieces of driftwood were strung together drawing attention up to the otherwise simple lighting fixture hanging in the center of the ceiling. Old blue glass mason jars were scattered about the room on various shelves and tables and were filled with a collection of sea glass and shells evidently plucked from the nearby beach. Emily's contribution to the room could be seen mostly within the built-in bookcases where her collection of the classics sat alongside the framed photos of her and Chase taken throughout the years they were together. On top of the fireplace mantel, leaning against the wall, was a large oval mirror incased in a square creamy-white wooden frame. The ornate frame was adorned with flowers and medallions and had been a birthday gift given to her by Chase.

A stack of *Coastal Living* magazines sat upon the coffee table beside a large Nantucket basket filled with dried flowers. The side tables, which were topped with simple glass lamps, also held smaller versions of the basket and held a collection of rusty items evidently found on the beach.

The wall opposite the fireplace held a section of dune fencing, secured to the wall with nautical rope. Hanging from the fencing were a variety of small watercolor paintings framed in driftwood along with netted glass fishing floats in shades of blue and green. Small wooden pegs held an assortment of items that had likely washed ashore, from tarnished spoons and broken toys to bits and pieces of broken china gathered in pieces of netting that appeared quite old.

Satisfied with all she had accomplished, Emily decided to shower and turn in for the night however, glancing at her watch she was surprised to see that it was only 8:30 and decided instead to order pizza before jumping in the shower to scrub off the dirt and fatigue she felt from the hours spent unpacking.

Chapter 7

Positioning the little wooden dingy just outside the cove, Riley was able to see, not only the cottage and dock, but also the section of the driveway that circled the front of the property where Emily parked her car. He had "borrowed" the boat from the dock where he worked having seen it sit there untouched throughout the week before. Evidently it belonged to the owners of one of the sailboats docked in the harbor as a means to transport them to and from their larger vessel. The majority of the boats was weekend toys for the rich businessmen in the area and sat unused throughout the workweek.

Working the third shift enabled him to hop on the boat and row the short distance early enough to watch Emily as she drove away from the cottage each morning. The money might be enticing, but he wasn't willing to end up back in corrections for *the man* and so, he had come out here every morning for a week to make sure she kept to a schedule. Riley would watch her leave the cottage at 9:30 sharp each morning before he would row back to the dock and walk the short distance to his apartment to get some sleep. At 5:00 he would return to the dock and row back over to the cove and wait until he saw her car pull in about 6:00. By 6:30 he was back in Newport and at the club drinking by 7:00.

Now certain that he could get in and do what needed to be done, Riley watched as Emily got into her car and drove away from the cottage.

"Time to move," he said to himself as he rowed the boat into the little cove and tied it to the dock.

Riley had worked for *the man* for the past thirty years off and on and though he was certain he could have hired a private investigator to do the jobs, he had always come back to Riley. The first time he had approached him, he had been standing outside the club smoking a cigarette. *The man* had driven up in his black sedan and offered Riley a hundred dollars just to talk. He had tossed his cigarette to the ground and was about to walk back into the club thinking the guy was some sort of pervert looking for something he wasn't about to give when *the man*, sensing his disgust assured him it would be worth his while. Figuring he could beat the guy senseless if he needed to, Riley grabbed the hundred-dollar bill and got into the car. It had turned out, all *the man* wanted was for Riley to tail a guy for a week and let him know what he did and where he went. Having no work and nothing better to do at the time, Riley had agreed and *the man* had rewarded him generously.

After that, *the man* had disappeared and Riley hadn't seen him for another two years. Then, once again, *the man* had shown up unexpectedly at the club where he walked in, nodded to Riley and walked back out to wait for him in his car. This time he wanted him to ask around about a piece of property, to see if he could find out anything about the owners.

Riley had no idea why this guy wouldn't hire a professional, but the money was good and he wasn't about to question his motives. Riley had asked around and found out that the property had been built and owned by an elderly couple. Despite fears that his lack of information would put an end to his business dealings with *the man*, he was surprised when over the next several years he was hired on several occasions to merely keep an eye on the property and report back.

As he approached the back porch that had remained unchanged for the past three decades, Riley felt the rush of adrenaline he always felt when he did a job. Technically there wasn't anything illegal about what he had done over the years, after all, private eyes did it all the time, but still, he often wondered what would happen if the cops showed up unexpectedly and because of that, he always felt a little anxious.

As always, the back door to the cottage was unlocked. The privacy of the property as well as the community itself gave owners little reason to consider themselves at risk and rarely locked their homes or their cars. Little had changed in the cottage from what he recalled and Riley wondered if perhaps the new woman living here now was somehow related to the woman who had lived here half a dozen years ago. Riley had no idea what connection the cottage had to *the man* and frankly didn't care as long as the money kept coming.

In the past, *the man* had hired him to look for things out of the ordinary. Anything that might seem out of place or indicate any unusual activity. Riley had never found anything of the sort. As far as he was concerned it was a simple cottage, with simple furnishings and modest taste, something even he could afford if it wasn't located on the shore. It seemed that the property itself was the only real thing of value given the multi-million dollar price tags for beachfront property on the island. Still though, *the man* had insisted that there had to be more to it than that and had urged Riley to consider everything as a potential explanation.

This time though, *the man* wanted more. This time he wanted Riley to search the property in a way he never had. To look for loose floorboards that might reveal a hiding place, to move large pieces of furniture to see if there might be sections cut out of the walls, to pry open a portion of the porch to see if there was anything buried beneath it. This was the first time he had been asked to do any sort of physical labor, but again, the money was too good to pass up.

He had come prepared with a small scoop shovel and a pickaxe. Walking the perimeter of each room and working his way inward, he first tested the floorboards for weak joints and inconsistencies. Finding nothing out of the ordinary, he moved on to the walls, pushing furniture about in search of hidden entry points. He was just about to start checking the half dozen closets when he heard a car pull into the gravel driveway. Grabbing the pickaxe lying on the floor, he bolted for the bedroom window, jumping out onto the back porch just as he heard the front door open. Slithering over the railing he crouched down behind a hydrangea bush cursing himself for leaving the shovel lying carelessly by the back door.

"Damn it." He whispered to himself as he peered over the bush, holding his breath that she didn't come out and find it. He listened intently as she moved about the kitchen apparently fixing her lunch. Deciding he had better risk it, he cautiously moved around the bush and climbed the three steps to the porch, remaining crouched down so that she wouldn't see him through the window. Grabbing the shovel he retreated back to the side of the cottage before darting toward the tree line on the side of the property, stopping only when he was safely out of sight.

"Shit!" He said as he realized he had left the boat tied to the dock, something she was sure to notice once she came outside. *Shit, shit, shit. Of all the stupid things to do.* Why hadn't he left it on the edge of the cove, hidden in the dunes? Tossing the shovel and axe on the ground he made a mad dash back to the side of the cottage and again listened. She was now in the bedroom where he could hear her opening and closing bureau drawers while she hummed to the radio playing in the kitchen.

The ringing of her cell phone practically made him jump out of his skin. Clearly the phone was lying on the bed next to the open window.

"Hello..." she answered, "That sounds great, I was just about to jump in the shower; I'll see you in a bit."

Grabbing her clothes she headed in the direction of the bathroom.

Breathing a deep sigh of relief, Riley waited until he heard the shower turn on before running to the dock, untying the rope and rowing as fast as he could out of sight. He would leave the shovel and axe where they were. He would be back, but next time he wouldn't be so stupid.

Chapter 8

Checking the time on her cell phone for at least the sixth time in half an hour, Emily nervously paced back and forth in front of the restaurant where she had agreed to meet Philip Bohman. She had been unable to come up with a legitimate excuse to avoid what was sure to be an uncomfortable dinner laced with long awkward silences and the rehashing of memories best left in the past, so she had just resolved to get it over with as quickly as possible.

Every since the day of his unexpected call at the shop, she had been thinking about Chase's funeral. As the only relatives of Chase she had ever met were his grandparents and his grandmother had passed away shortly after her daughter Sarah, Emily had contacted his grandfather Chester Eastwick to relay the sad news of his unexpected passing. Chester had been gracious enough to handle all the arrangements for the service to allow her the time to grieve. She would never be able to thank him enough for the gesture as well as his kind words during the Eulogy where he expressed his gratitude to her for making Chase's last years the happiest years of his life and that though he had not lived long enough to officially make her a part of the family, as far as he was concerned, Chester would always think of her as the granddaughter he never had.

Philip, she recalled, was a different story entirely. Though he had attended the service, he had sat in the back of the church away from the family and friends that had gathered to say goodbye to Chase. When the gathering had moved to the cemetery, Emily couldn't help but notice that Philip stood apart from the family, something that didn't go unnoticed by Chester who stood by Emily's side, his arm draped over her shoulder. After seeing her to the car that would take her back to his estate for a catered lunch with their closest friends, Emily watched as Chester quietly but firmly scolded Philip for his behavior and sent him on his way. She was not surprised when he did not attend the gathering at the house.

She had expected to hear from him in the days following the service, perhaps to invite her to meet privately to explain his actions, but the call had never come. Eventually she had let it go, realizing that everyone had their own way of grieving and thinking that perhaps he was overcome with guilt at having never really gotten to know the man that was his son.

Swallowing the lump in her throat that was threatening to choke her, Emily took a deep breath and tried to calm her emotions so that she could get through this uncomfortable meeting. Spotting the familiar man approaching the building she raised her hand to say hello in case he didn't recognize her.

"Mr. Bohman, I'm Emily, it's nice to finally meet you." She said extending her hand to shake his.

"Please...call me Philip, Mr. Bohman was my Father." He responded, grasping her hand for a firm yet gentle shake. Stepping in front of her, he opened the door for Emily and gave his name to the hostess who checked her list before showing them their table in a quite corner of the restaurant.

While the staff filled their water glasses and took their drink orders, they smiled pleasantly at each other across the small table.

"I apologize for not being available to meet with you sooner," Emily said, interrupting the uncomfortable silence. "Since I opened the bookstore I've been working seven days a week, but I finally got around to hiring a couple of people to help me out and give me a little free time."

"Of course... I understand. As I said when I phoned you, I had been meaning to contact you for quite some time. It's been difficult for me to come to grips with the loss of my son. I'm sure you know we were never very close. That being said...I feel a great sense of loss as well as guilt for not having put my family first." Avoiding eye contact with her, he focused on the bourbon he swirled in his glass.

Emily wasn't sure how to respond other than acknowledge his statement.

"I'm sure Chase loved you very much, he was a good man. I never heard him say a negative word in regards to his family."

"I'm glad to hear that." Philip said, finally looking into her eyes. "I have to admit, I was a bit hurt when I heard that he had left you the property in Jamestown. I had hoped it would remain in the family."

"Oh..." Emily suddenly felt the cold demeanor Chase had often referred to when describing his conversations with his Father. "Chase and I had planned on moving in shortly before his accident, in fact, that was why he was out there in the first place. He had many fond memories of the cottage as well as his summers with his aunt and he wanted to share that with me." She paused allowing Philip time to consider Chase's motive. "I'm sure he never intended to hurt you, you are more than welcome to come by as often as you like."

Philip sat silently, reflecting on what she had said. "I don't suppose you would be willing to sell." He proposed, again looking her directly in the eyes.

"I'm sorry...Mr. um Philip...I don't wish to hurt your feelings or to insinuate that I have more of a right to the property than you do, and as I said you are more than welcome any time, but right now it's my only connection to Chase. When I'm there I feel like he's with me and it's not something I'm willing to give up at this time. I'm not ready to move on yet. I hope you understand." She reached across the table to place her hand on top of his, a gesture intended to assure him that her motives, although selfish were one of love for his son.

Though he didn't pull away, Emily could feel the tension in his hand and frantically sought to change the subject.

"So tell me what's good here." She said, opening the menu and feigning interest, though they had clearly both lost their appetites.

An hour later after a dinner laced with small talk, the pair parted ways. Emily again invited Philip to come by the cottage any time he wished and he thanked her before stating that his offer to buy the property would remain open if she ever changed her mind.

When Emily arrived back in Jamestown she was completely exhausted and hoped Philip wouldn't take her up on her offer, at least for a while. By the time she had showered and gotten into bed she was convinced the sole purpose of the get-together had been an attempt to con her out of her inheritance. Perhaps she should speak to Chester regarding the matter to see if he too felt slighted by Chase's decision or whether it was Philip alone that felt cheated.

Chapter 9

Cupping his chin, Riley dragged his dirty nails through the stubble that was slowly taking over his usually clean-shaven face. Exhausted from working the third shift and then rowing out to the edge of the cove to once again watch the woman leave for work, Riley fought to stay awake long enough to secure the boat to a nearby tree branch to await her return. Her unexpected arrival in the middle of the day had been too close for comfort and he wasn't about to let it happen again. He had been lucky that time, chances were, he wouldn't be again.

Having expressed his concerns to *the man* when he stopped by the club for an update, he had been surprised at *the man's* understanding of the close call and was even more taken aback when he told Riley to take his time and make sure he was able to thoroughly check the place out. *The man* was adamant that he be careful to put everything back in the same place so that the woman was unaware that anything had been disturbed. If, he said, she did catch him on the property, he was to pretend to be a local fisherman and unaware that he was trespassing on private property.

The woman, he said, was not to be scared or harmed in any way.

Riley decided the only way to make sure he wasn't interrupted was to watch her for a week to determine what her exact schedule was. This was the fifth day of doing just that and Riley was really feeling the impact that the lack of sleep as well as the decrease of alcohol in his system was having on him. Not only was he physically exhausted, but he was extremely edgy, something that had not gone unnoticed by his coworkers. Twice this week he had nearly been fired when he got into it with a couple of ex-cons on the dock. It was stupid shit that normally wouldn't have pissed him off, but under the circumstances had caused him to overreact and threaten the guys with the knife he was using to gut the fish.

Because it was difficult to get workers, his boss tended to look the other way when it came to the small stuff, but threatening another worker with a knife to his throat was over the top even for this industry and Riley was promised his next outburst would be his last. He hated the work; coming home reeking of fish guts, the smell so potent it clung not only to his clothes but his skin and hair as well. He could shower in perfume for a month and never get the stink off him. Luckily, the type of women guys like him attracted didn't seem to mind, so long as their drinks were paid for. Besides, it wasn't like he was going to do this for the rest of his life, just until he was able to score a job big enough to afford himself a ticket out of New England. Hopefully, he thought as he settled back in the boat for a quick nap, this job would do just that.

The hot summer sun made it difficult to get comfortable and by 11:00, after having relieved himself off the side of the boat and eating the sandwich he had brought, washing it down with a beer he kept cold hanging from a fishing line into the cool water, Riley decided he was confident enough with the woman's schedule to risk resuming his search. Rowing the boat to the edge of the property and stashing it behind a clump of trees, he walked to where he had dumped the shovel and pickaxe the week before and headed for the cottage.

Still on edge from his prior close encounter, he decided to stick to the outside of the property and quickly got to work prying a plank of wood on the side of the porch off so that he could crawl underneath. If the woman came home while he was under the porch it would be easy enough to prop up the board and remain hidden until he was able to make a run for cover. Reaching into his back pocket, he grabbed the small flashlight he kept with him and turned it on, illuminating the crawlspace lined in dirt and gravel. As with many of the cottages along the shore, the structure had no basement but instead stood atop pilings made from wood encased by cement cylinders.

Some of the homes in the area had enclosed the base of their homes while others chose to keep the area accessible for storage of kayaks, fishing poles and other water sports equipment. This home's owner had chosen to enclose the area, most likely to keep wild animals from taking up residence, making it much more difficult for Riley to move about.

Working his way from the perimeters of the structure to the middle, he crawled on his hands and knees, stopping every few paces to move about the soil. After an hour or so, with sweat and dirt caked to his face and neck, he was about to call it quits when his flashlight reflected on what appeared to be glass under what was most likely the master bedroom. Crawling slowly over to the area, he again directed his flashlight on the object, moving the soil to unearth a pair of woman's eyeglasses. Slipping the glasses into his pocket he crawled back to the opening he had made on the side of the porch and retrieved the shovel and pickaxe before returning to the spot.

Lying on his side he was able to move the shovel back and forth across the area, gently removing bits of soil until his shovel hit something solid. Again getting on his hands and knees, Riley dropped the shovel and reached for the pickaxe, tugging at the object until it was freed from the soil. Shining the light on the object, Riley's jaw dropped as he took in the human skull.

Leaving the tools and the skull where they laid, Riley made his way to the opening, his heart pounding in his chest.

"What the hell have you gotten yourself into?" He asked himself, looking around quickly before he made a dash for the tree line and the safety of the boat. With his hands shaking, he fumbled with his cell phone, searching for the number *the man* had given him in case of emergencies. While he waited for his employer to pick up, he breathed deeply in an attempt to steady his pounding heart.

"This had better be important." *The man* answered gruffly.

"It is..." Riley responded, struggling to get a hold of himself. "I just found a human skull under the cottage! What the hell did you get me into?" He demanded as his emotions turned from panic to anger.

"Where are you now?" *The man* asked, obviously not surprised by the discovery.

"I'm still here...on the boat...what do you want me to do?" Riley asked, hoping *the man* would suggest he go to the club and get a drink.

"Go back...keep digging and see what else you find. I suspect you might find more than one body. Don't call me again, I'll meet you later...7:00 outside the club." Without saying goodbye *the man* disconnected the call, leaving Riley staring at the cottage in the distance and wondering once more what the guy's connection was to the property and what he hoped to find.

Against his better judgment and after downing a couple more beers to steady his nerves, Riley returned to the cottage and resumed his search. After uncovering the remains of what appeared to be the rest of a woman by the shreds of clothing that still clung to her bare bones, Riley laid on his back to rest. Now that his eyes had adjusted to the surrounding area and the sun was low enough to shine through the opening he had made on the side of the porch, Riley could clearly see that someone had cut a section of flooring out and later replaced it.

"So that's how you did it." Riley said to himself. He had wondered how someone could have dug a hole in the tight space to bury the body. Obviously, whoever had killed the woman had cut a hole into the bedroom floor to stand in while digging. It would be easy enough to toss the body inside the hole without having to leave the safety of the house and possibly being seen by anyone passing by on the water.

Resuming the search, Riley continued to move the dirt and gravel away from the body until his shovel came into contact with another hard object. Using his hands to brush aside the dirt, he was able to unearth a second body, this one a male. Lifting the bones from the waist, what was once a pocket to a pair of trousers separated from the bones to reveal a wallet. Grabbing the wallet, Riley laid on his back, placing his small flashlight between his teeth and pulling the leather apart. A driver's license from the early 1970s revealed the elderly man to be a resident of the property he was now buried on.

Looking over to the first remains he had uncovered, Riley could only assume that she was his wife. He wasn't sure what *the man* was hoping to find, but as far as he was concerned, his work here was done. Sticking the wallet in the breast pocket of his shirt, Riley grabbed the shovel and pickaxe and crawled back out through the porch opening, securing the board back into place before heading back to the shelter of the trees and the boat that awaited him.

Chapter 10

For the first time in over two years, Emily had woken this morning without feeling the weight of the world on her shoulders and the heaviness in her heart that had become her self-imposed prison. It had been nearly a month since she had moved into the little cottage and she was finally settled in enough to invite her girlfriends over for a day fun and relaxation.

She had planned ahead, arranging for her employees to cover the entire weekend at the shop so that she would have all Saturday to prepare, allowing her plenty of time to clean, prepare the menu and shop. The forecast was calling for clear skies, mid 80's and a gentle breeze and for once, the weatherman had been right on the money. Emily had decided to go with a light menu with a Mexican theme and had prepared a homemade salsa and chips and a roasted corn and bean salad ahead of time as well as prepping the ingredients for tacos and quesadillas, which they would make when they were ready to eat. She had stopped at the liquor store and picked up ice, tequila and margarita mix as well as a six-pack of hard lemonade that was her friend Cara's favorite drink. Since no menu was complete without some form of chocolate, Emily had made a batch of brownies that she planned to top with coffee ice cream for dessert.

Glancing at her watch she realized she had been so excited about the day she had awakened much earlier than she had anticipated and found that she was without anything to do for the next two hours until her friends were due to arrive. Pouring herself a glass of orange juice, Emily strolled into the living room and picked up the old photo albums she had pulled out for reminiscing with her friends and began to flip through the pages of her past.

Cara and Emily had been friends since the first grade when they were both in the same Brownie Troop. Even all these years later, the freckle-faced girl with the curly red hair brought a smile to Emily's face. There was something about Cara's crooked smile that always made it look like she was up to no good and drew people in like a magnet. Everyone that met her said the same thing, they weren't sure why, but they were intrigued by her very presence and felt compelled to find out more about her. Though she had charmed many men over the years, her stubborn Irish personality had ultimately been her downfall and she hadn't met a man yet that was willing to take a backseat to her strong will. This suited Cara just fine since she wasn't looking to settle down any time soon. She enjoyed adventure and the risk of the unknown far too much to consider giving up even a little of her freedom.

Victoria—or Vicky, as she preferred to be called—was Emily's other best friend. Chase had introduced her to Vicky shortly after they had starting dating. Vicky was the girlfriend, now wife of Chase's best friend Aiden, who was a History professor at Brown. Emily smiled recalling the first time she met the couple. She and Chase were having dinner at an Italian restaurant on Federal Hill in Providence when the couple had approached the table. After introducing her to his friends he had suggested they meet up later at a little café on the East Side for coffee and dessert. Several months later, Chase had admitted that the "chance" encounter had been prearranged so that his buddy could advise him as to whether or not he had made a good choice, given his history of failed relationships. Chase had eased her worries by telling her that she had gotten two thumbs up and that both Aiden and Vicky had insisted he not screw this one up.

Emily and Vicky had quickly become friends and Cara was eager to meet the girl Emily often referred to as Cara's doppelganger, insisting the two were separated at birth and that Vicky was the good one while Cara was the bad. Unlike Cara who was suspicious of everyone and was always looking for flaws in people, Vicky was trusting to the point that people close to her often had to warn her about those people that might take advantage of her kind and generous nature. Emily was the voice of reason that balanced out the trio and between the three of them, there was no limit to what they might accomplish when they set out to do something.

The sound of a car pulling up to the front of the cottage interrupted Emily's reverie and she jumped up from the couch to great her guests, dumbfounded by the passage of time that she had lost while reflecting on the past. Getting to the front door just as the doorbell rang she flung open the door, her big grin disappearing as she faced Chase's father rather than her expected guests.

Struggling to hide her shock she stammered, "Mr. Bohman... I uh...I was expecting someone else."

Her obvious discomfort did not go unnoticed by Philip who took advantage of her shock to step past her into the cottage, uninvited.

"I hope I'm not interrupting," he said, looking about the room as if searching for some sort of scandalous activity that might be taking place within the confines of the quant abode.

"No...um...actually I am expecting a couple of friends." She stuttered, looking at her watch without actually registering the time. "Is there something I can do for you?"

"I was in town," He said over his shoulder as he turned his back to her and wandered over to the old chair. "I just thought I would stop by and see what you had done with the old place. It doesn't seem as if much has changed over the years."

His entitled attitude as well as his unannounced appearance put Emily's defenses on alert and she suddenly felt anxious to get rid of him.

"Normally," She said, keeping a firm hand on the doorknob, "I wouldn't mind you stopping by, but I am actually expecting company and still have a great deal to do. I hope you don't think me rude to suggest we reschedule the visit. Perhaps you could give me a call and we could arrange something that would work for both of us."

"Of course," Philip said, before rising from his seat, "I look forward to it." Taking a few steps forward he stopped in front of her, close enough that she could feel his breath as he spoke. "I don't suppose you've given any thought to my offer to buy the property?"

"No, Mr. Bohman, I haven't." Emily said firmly, pulling back her shoulders and standing rigid in order to emphasize her stance. "You will be the first to know if I do." She smiled warmly.

"Good day, Emily." Philip said, stepping past her through the front entry without waiting for her response.

As she watched him get in his car and leave, Emily couldn't help but feel a bit unnerved by the whole experience and an hour later when Cara and Vicky finally arrived, she was still mulling over the possible motives Philip might have for wanting the property. Putting a smile on her face and shaking off the anxiety the unexpected visit had brought, Emily rushed to the door to meet her friends.

"Welcome to my humble abode," she announced, sweeping her arm out to gesture them into the room. Once inside, the girls hugged and complimented each other on how wonderful they all looked.

"Okay, well, let me give you the grand tour." Emily said, stepping back from the women to conduct the tour. "This is the living slash dining area, as you can see…"

Ten minutes later the trio were blending frozen margaritas in the little kitchen and giggling like grade school kids. After pouring the drinks Emily suggested they go out back to the dock where she had set up three chaise lounge chairs facing out to the cove. Once they were settled in and the ladies had taken in the charming beauty of the place, Cara asked what she had been wondering since they arrived.

"So how are you doing, Emily…really?"

"I'm doing great, why do you ask?"

"Honestly…you seem a little distracted. Are you sure loving here was the right decision?"

"Oh no…yes. Let me start over. I am a little distracted, but it doesn't have anything to do with being here, not really."

"Well, that certainly clears things up." Vicky said sarcastically, elbowing Cara who nodded in agreement.

"Okay, number one, yes it was definitely the right decision to move here. I love the peaceful location, it's close to the shop and it helps me stay connected to Chase. I feel like he's here with me and it's comforting. Number two; I guess I am a bit distracted. Chase's father has contacted me a couple of times and popped by unexpectedly about an hour before you two arrived. He seems overly interested in buying the property from me."

"Why would he want it, didn't his wife die here?" Vicky asked, recalling Chase telling her and Aiden about the drowning. From what she remembered it was never determined whether the drowning was accidental or a suicide. Either way, she wouldn't think her husband would want to relive it every day.

"That's what bothers me," Emily thought out loud, "he didn't really explain why he wanted the property, just that he thought it should stay in the family."

"That's a little insulting." Cara interrupted, sitting up straight in her chair. "You are more family than Mr. Bohman will ever be and Chase spent more time here than he did. Besides, Chase gave it to you, not him. If I were you Emily I would do a little digging, ask around to see why he really wants the property."

"I wouldn't know where to start." Emily said thoughtfully. "Believe me, I would love nothing more than to never see the man again, but something tells me he's not going to give up that easily and that's what worries me. I was thinking about Chase's grandfather. He has a lot of connections around here, plus he might know something that I don't know. I just don't want to upset him."

"I think that's a great idea Emily." Cara said, patting her friend on the shoulder. "He was very kind to you when Chase passed, I'm sure he would want you to tell him if something didn't seem right. Now, let's take a dip, this water is calling to me." Without hesitation, Cara stood up from her chair, peeled off her cover-up and dove off the deck only to resurface shrieking about the temperature of the water.

After a cool swim, the ladies moved the party to the porch where they ate and drank while gossiping about just about everyone the three of them knew. By the time they said their goodbyes and Cara and Vicky drove out of sight, Emily had all but forgotten Philip's unexpected visit and the uneasy feelings his presence drew.

Chapter 11

Philip sat behind his oversized desk staring at the decanter of bourbon across the room.

"Screw it." He said, pushing back his chair and moving toward the liquor that was calling to him. It was far too early in the day to start drinking, but then again, why not. He had been stupid to go to the cottage uninvited. He had let his emotions get the best of him and tossed reason out the window. Now, he was certain that Emily was suspicious of his motives and he needed to think fast to rectify the situation.

As he drank his bourbon and stared out the window he considered whether or not it would be a good idea to call Emily and apologize for his intrusion. He could tell her that the death of his son had brought back memories of his long-lost wife and he simply wanted to be close to her. Certainly she would sympathize with him. On the other hand, wasn't that exactly why she insisted on keeping the property? Perhaps he should simply send her a note apologizing for his irrational behavior and back off for a little while.

"Damn it." He muttered, "There has to be some way I can..." All of the sudden, as if someone had smacked him on the back of the head, it dawned on him. Why hadn't he thought of this before? Grabbing a piece of letterhead from his desk, he smiled to himself at how easy it would be to convince Emily to go along with his plan without revealing the truth. Using the fountain pen Katherine herself had given him, he scribbled the note:

Dearest Emily,
I must apologize for intruding yesterday and hope that my unannounced visit was not too upsetting to you.

The truth is, that every since the loss of my son I have been burdened by deep feelings of regret, not only for his loss, but for that of my wife. Though she has been gone for over 30 years, I still feel her beside me each day. My fondest memories of her are the times we shared at the cottage and on the beach.

When we found Katherine's lifeless body, caught between the rocks on the shore, she was missing an antique ring I had given her that had been passed down by my family. It was my gift to her on our wedding day. The truth is, I have never stopped hoping that someday I would find that ring and that dream has kept me going all these years. Even after Sarah took over the property I would often go out there on weekends to search for the ring. I still have hope that one day it will be found.

Besides from Sarah, I have never told anyone about my quest for fear that they would think me a foolish man. I had hoped by purchasing the property from you, my secret would remain in tact, but I now realize that I should have trusted you enough to know you would understand. We are not that different, you and me. We both need the comfort of objects to keep our memories of those we lost alive.

I hope that in time you will be able to forgive me for being so foolish and perhaps one day you would be willing to allow me to continue my quest.

Yours truly,
Philip Bohman

As he folded the letter and placed it in an envelope, Philip smiled smugly at himself, certain that Emily would call him before the week was over encouraging him to resume his search.

Chapter 12

As he absently stirred his coffee while starring vacantly at the *Wall Street Journal* in front of him, Chester's thoughts were focused on his earlier conversation with Emily. He had been pleasantly surprised by her phone call suggesting they meet for dinner later in the week and had quickly agreed, suggesting a location close to her shop in Newport so that he might drop by there first; something he had been meaning to do since she opened it earlier in the year. Now, however, he wondered if perhaps there might be something more behind the invitation other than just wanting to get together to reminisce about his late grandson. In retrospect there had been a note of unease in Emily's voice and if the past had taught him anything; he was certain that Philip had something to do with it.

Chester would never forgive himself for allowing his daughter to marry a man he knew had ulterior motives. He had spent countless hours attempting to convince her not to go through with the wedding, but the more he pushed, the more she wanted him. In hindsight he should have feigned indifference to the marriage and he was certain Katherine would have quickly lost interest. Although he had loved his daughter, he was not blind to her games and had watched many a man; some of whom would have given their life for her, be tossed to the side with no thought to their feelings simply because she was bored of them or had her sights on another. It was only because of his disapproval that Philip had captured her hand in marriage, and he had no one to blame but himself. Even his late wife had begged him to back off, but his intense abhorrence for Philip was simply too overwhelming and he stubbornly refused to listen to reason.

Now, over thirty years later, when his wife and his daughters were gone, he was left alone with the constant reminder of the biggest regret of his life. Many times he had considered firing Philip and tossing him out on the streets and out of his life, but his need to prove that his daughter's death had not been an accident and that Philip had murdered her, outweighed his hatred for the man and so he continued his efforts to prove his theories without revealing his suspicions to anyone.

A knock at the door of his office brought Chester out of his reverie and he looked up to see Philip standing in the doorway, waiting to be invited in. Fighting back the urge to tell him how he really felt, Chester motioned for Philip to enter the office.

"Good morning, Sir." Philip said, moving closer to the desk while waiting for Chester to offer him a seat.

"Philip." Chester responded, barely acknowledging his presence while he flipped the pages of the newspaper he wasn't really reading.

Philip stood silently for a moment, waiting for his father-in-law to give him his attention, but the uncomfortable silence seemed to stretch beyond the confines of the room and Philip grew irritated.

"I was wondering whether you had heard that I met with Greg Sinclair last week and sealed a deal for a showcase at this year's Boat Show. Excursion Charters will be the only charter company to be featured. I thought we might discuss some marketing ideas."

Chester leaned back in his chair, looking at Philip for the first time since he entered the room.

"Good Lord, Philip, straighten your tie. You look like you just got out of bed. I shouldn't have to remind you that; as a representative of this company you need to present yourself with a style parallel to that of our product. No one wants to commission a vessel from a man who looks like he just walked out of a pub."

Philip gritted his teeth as he straightened his tie, all the while stuttering, "Yes Sir, of course...my apologizes."

"Very well." Chester nodded, delighted that he had rattled the man, "Work up some samples of what you have in mind with the Marketing Department. I trust you haven't come to me without some sort of vision in mind?"

"Yes, of course Sir. I should have something ready to show you by the end of the week. Shall we meet on Friday?"

"See my secretary on your way out, she will fit you in if I'm available." Without saying goodbye, Chester returned his gaze to the newspaper, dismissing Philip with a wave of his hand.

As the door clicked shut, Chester stifled a chuckle. He so enjoyed toying with Philip. His constant need for approval only encouraged Chester's condemnation of even his most notable accomplishments. If he couldn't rid himself of the untrustworthy scoundrel, the least he could do was make every moment they spent together a living hell for him.

Chapter 13

Emily tossed back the covers, stretching lazily before climbing out of bed. There was a dampness to the morning air that indicated the threat of a storm on the horizon. Pulling back the sheer curtains that clung to the tacky windowpane, she surveyed the dark sky as well as the rough sea. The humidity engulfed everything around her including the floorboards where she stood barefooted. As she lifted her feet to walk she could feel the tackiness of what remained of the polyurethane on the old wood. Despite the uncomfortable heat and the approaching storm, she had a lot to do around the cottage and it appeared by the trickle of sweat running down her lower back, the sooner she got started the better.

Now that she was completely moved in, it was time to start weeding through the remainder of Sarah's belonging to see if there was anything that should be returned to her father. Chase had removed a number of large items when he had decided to make use of the property, boxing up the smaller bits and pieces to go through at a later time and storing them in the limited closet space. As much as she had managed to downsize her essentials, Emily still lacked the space to store the remaining garments she held in her storage unit and she wanted to retrieve them before they were damaged by the elements. Though the space was large enough to store whatever she couldn't part with, it wasn't temperature controlled, so until she could afford to build a garage she wanted to minimize the number of items at risk.

Pulling on a pair of shorts and a tank top, Emily moved to the bathroom to wash her face and tie her hair up in a sloppy bun. It was days like this that made her want to cut it short, something she had done in the past, only to regret it later. It was much easier to work with long hair that could be pulled up in a ponytail then to have to stand under a hot hairdryer in the middle of a summer heat wave in order to style a shorter cut. Satisfied that the messy bun would keep her hair off her already sweaty neck, she returned to the bedroom and opened the tiny closet.

Somehow Chase had managed to jam at least a dozen boxes into the small space using both the floor of the closet as well as the shelf above the hanging rod, leaving Emily just enough room to hang a handful of summer tops and a half dozen sun dresses. Starting from the top, Emily removed the three boxes from the shelf and quickly dug through them; finding them to contain woman's clothing. The boxes had been marked "donate" on the sides and Emily agreed, carrying the boxes out to her car to drop off at Goodwill later in the day. Stopping in the kitchen to grab a tall glass of orange juice, she returned to the bedroom and pulled a box from the floor of the closet, which was marked "linens". Without removing the items from the box, Emily was able to see about half a dozen sets of sheets as well as a couple of old thermal blankets. Setting it aside for the time being, she decided that this box would join the others in her car for donation. The next few boxes were marked "books" and Emily dragged those into the living room to go through later. A small box in the corner of the closet marked "misc." drew her attention and she carried the box over to the bed to sift through it. Amongst scrapbooks and old yearbooks, Emily found an assortment of clipping from the local papers pertaining to the discovery of Katherine's body as well as several follow-up articles regarding the investigation. The clipping had been tucked into the pages of a copy of Ernest Hemingway's *The Old Man and the Sea.*

Inside the cover of the book was written – *To my dear sister, who finds adventure in every day of her life, Love, Katherine.*

Emily traced her finger over the beautifully written words and felt somehow cheated at not having known either of these women who were so important to the man she loved and missed. Feeling a lump swell in her throat she shook off the self-pity and placed the book, minus the clipping with the scrapbooks she intended to give to Chester. The remainder of the contents were ribbons Sarah had won for horseback riding as well as several letters bond together with a satin ribbon in faded lilac. Though she was curious about their content, they appeared to be deeply personal and she didn't feel she had earned the right to read them, having never actually met the woman. Returning the scrapbooks and Hemingway novel to the box, Emily placed it to the side and retuned to the closet.

The next three boxes were all marked "winter clothes" and after looking inside to confirm the contents she carried them along with the box of linens out to her car. By the time she shoved the last of the boxes into her back seat, the rain was coming down hard and there was a rumble of thunder in the distance. Quickly running back into the cottage, Emily returned to the bedroom where she retrieved the final two boxes from the floor of the closet. Both boxes were curiously marked "treasures" and Emily smiled thinking again of Chase and his stories from his childhood. Eager to see what was inside, Emily placed the two boxes up on her bed, kicked off her flip-flops and jumped up on the bed to get comfortable. Her heart pounded like a six-year-old on Christmas morning as she pulled the tape off the first box. Inside she found an assortment of rusty license plates that had apparently washed up on the beach, as well as several tangled wads of fishing line, complete with hooks and dried up seaweed. There were several plastic bags filled with bits of broken sea glass, each bag containing a different color. An old cigar box contained bits of broken jewelry, including a rusty watchband, several pieces of costume jewelry, all tarnished and broken as well as plastic beads and bubblegum machine rings. Returning the items to the box, Emily pushed it aside and opened the second and final box.

Emily stared in awe at what she saw. Unlike the first box, which was filled with junk washed ashore, this box contained what appeared to be actual items of value. Pulling out an old oil lantern, Emily studied it carefully, noting the hand-blown glass and heavy metal construction that indicated the piece was quite old. There was a decanter made out of clay as well as a bottle incased in sediment that had retained its wax seal. Shaking the bottle, Emily could hear the liquid still preserved within. A tin box contained more than a dozen coins, heavy in weight that appeared to be several hundred years old. Finally there was a piece of nautical rope still connected to an old piece of wood, perhaps belonging to a vessel long lost to the sea.

Emily sat transfixed by what she saw, wondering why Sarah had kept these items when clearly they held real historical value. Though it was unlikely that she would have sold the items for profit, from everything she had learned of the woman from Chase, she was surprised she hadn't donated them to one of the local museums. Uncertain what she should do with the find, Emily placed the box back into the closet and stood back to admire what she had accomplished.

With the closet now emptied of all but one box, she now had room to hang the clothes that were currently stored in bins under her bed. Though many of the items were in bad need of ironing, she decided to get them all hung and deal with that as she wore them. An hour later with the closet once again filled; only this time with her own belongings, Emily was satisfied with what she had accomplished and decided to take a quick shower before having lunch.

Once again clean, although still perspiring, Emily tossed a salad and poured herself a tumbler of sweet ice tea, which she carried into the living room to eat. The rain was still coming down hard and steady outside the cottage and the gray skies cast a gloomy shadow over the room. Switching on the table lamps, Emily took a couple bites of salad before digging into the first box containing books. It was easy to see where Sarah's passion lied as she pulled out several classics including *Treasure Island, Swiss Family Robinson, Moby Dick, The Odyssey* as well as *Robinson Crusoe.* The books appeared nearly new in condition and with identical covers, looked to be part of reproduction collection. Each book was bound in black leather and embossed with gold lettering. Though the reproductions held no value to a collector, they were still beautifully bound and Emily set the books aside to keep for herself. Next she found three books pertaining to nautical antiques and collecting, which she also set aside. Perhaps Sarah had researched her finds at one time. The remainder of the box contained a vast collection of *The Hardy Boy* books, perhaps read and belonging to Chase himself. These, she decided, she would donate to the local library to be enjoyed by a new generation of boys.

After finishing her salad and tea, Emily decided to brave the elements and drive out to the local Goodwill store to drop off the boxes that she had loaded into her car earlier. There was no point in going any further until she had room in her car to get rid of things. Besides, she still had all afternoon to go through the remaining closets and hopefully, she thought as she stepped out into the driveway; the rain would cool things off a bit.

Chapter 14

Riley looked around the grubby studio apartment one more time. After today he would never have to set foot in it again. That is, if *the man* came through on his end of the deal. It had been two days since they had met after he had discovered the bones under the cottage, and he was still pissed off.

He had waited outside the club that night, a backpack containing the few items he owned slung over his shoulder; when the dark sedan pulled up. After leaving the cottage he had returned to his tiny apartment just long enough to shower and grab his stuff. His palms had been itching every since, as he anxiously waited at the club for *the man* and the money he had promised him. He would ask the guy to drop him off at the bus station and decide from there where he wanted to go. Despite daydreaming for years about some day leaving the state and his pathetic life, he had never really settled on a specific destination. All he knew was that he wanted to go south. Beyond that, it didn't really matter to him where he hung his hat.

Riley opened the door to the sedan and got in, leaving one foot on the ground and the door slightly ajar; he extended his hand.

"Not so fast." *The man* said, shaking his head. "Get in."

"You better not be playing me...we had a deal." Riley said through gritted teeth.

Without responding the man waited for Riley to put his leg in the car and shut the door before he drove to a secluded corner of the parking lot, behind a dumpster. Putting the car in park, he reached into his suit coat and took out a long envelope.

"You will find half of what we agreed upon in there." He said, handing the envelope to Riley who quickly snatched it out of his hand.

"Half...what do you mean half? I did what you asked, now pay up." Riley leaned over grabbing *the man* by his jacket, ready and able to beat the shit out of him if he needed to.

"Settle down, you'll get the rest. There's one more thing I need you to do." Brushing Riley's hand away, he straightened his jacket before continuing.

"In the envelope you'll find a name and a phone number. Tomorrow morning I want you to call the man, his secretary will ask for your name; tell her it's a personal call. Tell her it's about the cottage in Jamestown. She will most likely put you on hold and check with him before putting you through. Once you're through tell him you know what he did...tell him you found the bodies under the porch. That's it, don't get cocky and add anything, just hang up. Call my phone when it's done. Once we're square I'll give you instructions on where you can pick up the rest of the money. Do you understand?"

"I got it." Riley muttered before opening his door and stepping out of the car. "This better be the end of it." Without waiting for a response he stuffed the envelope in his back pocket and walked back over to the club where he disappeared through the door into the smoke-filled bar.

He had done what *the man* asked, and it had gone down exactly as he had said it would. The secretary had asked for his name, he ignored her request and told her it was a personal call about the cottage. She had paused briefly before asking him to hold. Then a guy had answered the phone and he had repeated the words exactly as he had been instructed. Just before he hung up he could hear the guy demand to know who he was.

Next he had called *the man* and told him the job was done. He was advised to return to the club later that night and that he would find a locker key taped to the back of the dumpster. He would find his money in the corresponding locker at the bus station in Providence.

Though he half expected another stall and decided to leave his stuff behind, the key was there so he had stayed at the club to celebrate with a few beers before grabbing a cab back to his place. Asking the cabbie to wait, he grabbed his backpack which was lying on the floor next to the mat he called a bed. Now he gave once last glance before closing the door. As the cabbie drove, he rode in silence, hopeful that his shitty life was behind him and that he could finally make something of himself. His cynical nature told him to prepare for disappointment, for *the man* to screw him one more time, but he couldn't help but to cling on to the possibility that his hard work and loyalty to a man he didn't really know, had finally paid off.

After paying the cabbie, Riley once again slung the backpack over his shoulder and rushed eagerly into the bus station. Though it was nearly ten o'clock the station was bustling with activity. Stopping just inside the doors, Riley searched the perimeter looking for the lockers. Spotting a sign pointing to the location, Riley moved in its direction, ignoring several individuals; obviously hard up, soliciting money. Normally he would have shoved them aside, telling them to get a job, but right now all he could do was focus ahead on the lockers and hopefully the money he had earned. Approaching the lockers, Riley removed the key from his pocket, checking the number against the corresponding metal box. Taking a deep breath he opened the locker and reached inside, retrieving a small manila envelope. Hand written on the outside of the envelope it read simply "Thanks and good luck".

Looking around to make sure he wasn't being watched, Riley slowly opened the envelope. Inside he found a wad of hundred-dollar bills bond together with a rubber band.

Kneeling down to put the money in his backpack Riley smiled, *the man* was all right after all. It was a shame they hadn't met under different circumstances. Under his three-piece suits, the guy wasn't that much different from him. He might wear expensive clothes and drive a nice car, but Riley had been around long enough to know the difference from those that had been born to money and those that had inherited it and he would bet his life that the man was the latter.

Chapter 15

As the rain and wind continued to beat against the old windows of the cottage, Emily resumed her efforts to clear out the remaining closets. The second bedroom, which was barely large enough to fit its twin-size bed and nightstand, contained a cupboard comparable to that of a broom closet. Within the small space was a hanging rod no more than three feet in length below which was a set of drawers. Opening the drawers, Emily found several articles of clothing, which she could only assume belonged to Chase when he was a teenager. Removing a t-shirt from the pile, she held it up, smiling at the small size before holding it up to her face to breath in its scent. Disappointment creased her forehead as she acknowledged that the item held no trace of the cologne she missed so dearly.

Clearing the contents from the drawers quickly, as not to distract herself from the task at hand, Emily placed them in a box for donation and moved on to the hallway closet. Once again she noted that the cottage, though charming, was lacking in adequate storage space, thus the need to purge, not only Sarah's belongings, but all the unnecessary items of her own. This closet, it seemed, was used to store off-season items and contained a number of boots, coats as well as a wicker basket containing hats, gloves and winter scarves. Doubling as a broom closet, Emily found a mop, broom, dustpan as well as several cleaning rags. Leaving these items in place, she removed only the clothing items, setting aside a couple of pairs of gloves she found appealing.

The bathroom closet she knew held only a hamper, a shelf of towels and her own toiletries, having had rid it of everything else when she had first moved in, and so she moved on to the closet opposite the front door of the cottage. Covered with an old sheet, was a small artificial Christmas tree, still decorated and tucked away for future use. A plastic bin containing lights, stockings and other holiday decorations, visible through the plastic, rested on the only shelf beside a second bin containing what appeared to be fall decorations. Though it was evident there had been a hanging rod at one time it had been removed; probably to make room for the tree, and so a hook had been installed against the back of the closet to hold a lone umbrella.

The final closet was in the tiny kitchen beside the back door. Though she had been in the closet several times since moving in, she hadn't had the opportunity to really clean it out. More of a pantry cupboard than a closet, the space was lined with shelves. The shelves were perhaps four feet in length and equally as wide. Dragging a chair into the closet, Emily balanced herself, holding onto the top shelf for added comfort. Several dusty food storage containers lined the shelf as well as an assortment of small appliances including a bread maker, an electric can opener, a rice steamer and an old air popcorn machine. Removing the containers, Emily placed them on a lower shelf before stepping down from the chair. The remaining shelves contained a supply of dry goods, all well beyond their use by dates and Emily quickly filled a number of trash bags with the spoiled food. Everything that she hadn't placed on the shelves herself had to go and she easily completed the task just before a rumble of thunder followed by a bolt of lightening took out her power and left her in virtual darkness.

Stepping out of the closet, Emily grabbed a small flashlight from the counter and went in search of candles. Though it was still mid-afternoon, the dark skies cast an eerie glow on the tiny cottage and a shiver of nerves made the hair on her arms stand up in response. Though she considered herself quite brave in most circumstances, there was something about being alone in the middle of a storm on this lonely stretch of road that left her a little on edge. Having found and lit several small candles throughout the cottage, Emily returned to the kitchen to make herself a cup of tea. Thank goodness for gas stoves. While she waiting for the water to heat, her mind drifted back to a storm that had left her and Chase in the dark.

Unlike this summer storm, it was a January ice storm that had taken out several power lines that had left them, along with most of the city, in the dark. Several days of freezing rain had proved too much for the lines to bear and when the winds had picked up a bit, causing tree branches to sway against the already weighted lines, they began to fall like dominos. The Governor had declared it a state of emergency and had ordered all non-essential businesses to close, leaving them nothing to do but stay inside and enjoy each other's company.

For nearly four days they had stayed in bed, reading, talking and making love. Chase had entertained her with tales of his youth, most of which took place at this very cottage, while she expressed a longing to share adventures of equal merit with him in the future.

The whistle of the teakettle drew Emily from her reverie and she poured her tea and retreated to the comfort of the living room to wait out the storm. As if by divine intervention, the power flickered and came back on just as she was taking her last sip of tea. An audible sigh of relief escaped her lips and she sprung from the couch eager to resume her work and put the uneasiness behind her.

By the time she had removed the trash bags from the kitchen, placing them in the outside barrels and loaded the remaining boxes into her car, the storm had all but passed leaving nothing but wet sand and beach debris as a reminder of its strength. The day's humidity had passed and a calm breeze urged Emily to take a break from her work and walk along the shore. Kicking off her flip-flops and leaving them on the porch, Emily sunk her feet into the cool, wet sand and strolled to the water's edge. The shore was peppered with several small shells along with small sticks and other typical debris one might find after a storm. As she neared the rocks along the edge of the cove, her eyes fell upon an object that appeared to be wedged between several smaller rocks. Quickening her pace, Emily moved in to get a closer look. Searching the shore for something to use as a poker, she grabbed a branch that had fallen from a nearby tree during the storm. Relieving the branch of its leaves, Emily nudged the limb in between the rocks, loosening their grip on the object before reaching in and pulling out a small wooden box.

Dropping the branch, she placed the box carefully down on a boulder to examine it. Rather non-descript, the box appeared to be quite old, although Emily acknowledged that the elements may have accelerated its aging. The box looked to be made of solid oak and was perhaps the size of a cigar box. A latch securing the box's contents was made of brass and was again plain, lacking of detail or design. Using the side of her index finger, Emily easily lifted the latch and stared in awe at what she discovered.

Thrilled by her unexpected find Emily quickly returned to the cottage to examine the box and its contents more thoroughly. Once seated comfortably in the living room, Emily sifted through the stack of books still piled on the floor for the one pertaining to nautical antiques. Flipping through the pages she was quickly able to identify the object in the box as a tide and time clock. Lifting the heavy brass piece from the box, Emily studied the piece at length, hoping to find some way of dating the clock. Her lack of knowledge in the area made it difficult to determine anything other than the maker of the clock, which she considered might be the key to determining its possible age.

Anxious to find more treasure, Emily placed the piece back in the box and quickly returned to the spot where it was discovered, hoping to find anything else that might be trapped within the grouping of rocks.

Chapter 16

Straightening his tie and raking his hand through his gray hair, Chester studied his reflection thoughtfully. When had he gotten so old? It seemed like only yesterday that he was running through the streets barefooted, wearing nothing but a pair of trousers rolled up to his knees, carrying a homemade fishing pole in search of his buddies and the anticipation of an afternoon catch. Life was so simple back then, when the only thing he had to worry about was getting caught skipping school or running into one of his father's friends who might scold him and send him home.

His father was a proud man, ever recounting the sacrifices he had made to give his son the opportunities he never had. A businessman himself, Chester's father had opened up a small pub along Newport Harbor well before it was a trendy tourist town. In those days he made his money off the seamen that came ashore from the many fishing vessels that docked along the waterfront. Though some of the men had families, most were barely men at all and eager to spend their wages on cheap beer and even cheaper women. It wasn't the sort of business that brought the family social acceptance, no…they were considered no better than the men and women that frequented the pub. Chester's mother took in laundry, working hard to supplement their income as well as allowing her to rub elbows with some of the more respectable residents in town.

Chester flinched, thinking about how ashamed he had been of his family back then. He had turned his back on his parents and the business his father had left him. How ironic it was that the place he had once considered an anchor holding him down was now a successful hot spot frequented by the wealthiest and oldest Newport families. As a foolish young buck, straight out of the University, Chester had taken the first offer he got to rid himself of the business and everything it represented to him. Now, three generations later, the man's family still owned and operated the sophisticated establishment, which had awarded them enough profit to finance several additional businesses along the same stretch of sand.

Shaking off his regret and memories of the past, Chester turned from the mirror and stepped into the outer office, waving goodbye to his secretary who was busy transcribing minutes from the earlier board meeting. As he waited for the parking attendant to bring around his car, he phoned Emily, reconfirming their plans and advising her that he should arrive shortly at the shop. A smile passed his lips as he listened to her excited response on the other end of the call. He hadn't realized how eager he was to see her until he heard her voice.

Stopping by a local florist in route to the shop, Chester purchased an arrangement of pale apricot colored roses and baby's breath flowers placed inside an ornate crystal vase. Now within walking distance to both the shop and the restaurant he had made reservations at, Chester made his way through the maze of tourists flooding the streets as the shop owners closed their doors for the day. As he approached the bookstore, he couldn't help but feel a gentle tug at his heart seeing his grandson's name scrolled into the shop sign.

Oh, but if things could have been different, he thought, standing in front of the shop motionless while passerby's bumped his elbows nearly relieving him of the arrangement he cradled in his hands. Spotting him outside the shop, Emily rushed to open the door, which she had already locked to avoid dealing with last minute customers.

"Mr. er…Chester, do come in." She muttered, motioning for him to join her inside. "It's so nice to see you."

Exchanging a hug for the lovely arrangement she placed the flowers on top of the coffee table and gestured for him to follow her. Nearly a half hour later, Emily completed her tour of the shop, leading Chester to the small corner dedicated to Chase and his writings.

"I must say," Chester, announced, "I am very impressed by your selection of the classics. There aren't a great deal of shops like this that cater to the great writers of the past. Much of what is written now a day is pure dribble, junk food for the mind, not at all original in content. My grandson was one of the few modern writers who captured the imagination, if I might borrow the phrase from the name of your shop."

Emily laughed, "But of course." She obliged, curtsying with the grace and elegance of a ballerina after a performance. "I know that Chase would have been flattered while at the same time, embarrassed by the recognition, but honestly, it was his own passion for writing and his love of the classics that sold me on the idea. I didn't want the shop to be just another tourist trap, but by placing a few volumes pertaining to local topics in the window, I'm able to draw in readers that might not otherwise consider the value of these books." Emily took a deep breath, realizing that her enthusiasm was getting the best of her.

Chester reached out, taking her hand in his own. "I can see why my grandson was so taken with you." Patting her hand, he took one last glance around the shop. "Now…I don't know about you, but I'm starving…shall we?" He said, dropping her hand and offering his arm to escort her from the shop in gentlemanly fashion.

As they casually walked in the direction of the restaurant, Chester entertained Emily with a bit of a history lesson regarding some of the older establishments on the block. Though he spoke with confidence and obvious intelligence, Emily couldn't help but hear an undertone of local tongue, something that was only recognized by life-long residents themselves. As he continued to educate her concerning the turn of the century architecture, Emily's mind drifted to the letter she had received earlier in the day.

The letter had arrived with her regular mail at the shop and drew her attention by the return address. At first she had thought it might be a note from Chester, bowing out of their dinner plans and wondered briefly why he wouldn't just phone her to cancel. After reading the note from Philip she considered calling him, however decided instead to discuss the matter with Chester before agreeing to his request.

Emily's obvious distraction intrigued Chester and after ordering a bottle of wine and waiting for the waiter to leave their table, he reached out, once again placing his hand on top of her own.

"What is it, dear? Are my stories that bad that I have lost your attention completely?" He asked winking at her to let her know he was teasing.

"No...of course not...I'm sorry Chester. Perhaps I am a bit distracted." Emily apologized.

Filling Chester in regarding the unexpected visit and multiple requests to sell the property, Emily reached into her purse and withdrew the letter she had received from Philip.

After allowing him time to read the note, Emily sighed, "So you see, I'm not sure what to think. Is it true that there was a ring? I really don't know what to do."

Chester continued to stare at the letter, deep in thought until he was interrupted by the waiter returning with the wine and advising them of the evening specials. After ordering their meals and allowing the waiter to pour the wine before retreating to the kitchen, Chester finally spoke.

"It's no secret that I have never been fond of Philip. I have always thought that my daughter could have done much better and in fact may still be alive today if it weren't for him. That being said, I am grateful that he gave me a wonderful grandson whose memory I shall always cherish." Chester paused, considering his words carefully.

"There was a time that I suspected Philip of causing my daughter's death. Whether it was an accident or intentional I have never been sure. Either way, I was determined to find the truth. My hatred for the man consumed my life to the point that I vowed to never stop searching until I was able to find proof or get his confession. Now though, I have grown tired...tired of the game, tired of missing out on the pleasures in life while I continued to obsess over what might or might not have been. I'm not a young man. Who knows how many years I have left in this world? I refuse to allow Philip to consume me any longer."

Leaning back in his chair, Chester took a deep breath. "I'm afraid I may be a bit jaded in regards to Philip and what his intentions may be. Whether there was a ring, I couldn't say, though it's possible. My advice to you, dear, is to proceed with caution. If in fact there was a ring and it truly holds sentimental value to Philip, then I believe that Chase would have wanted him to have it. I would just keep in mind that if Philip is indeed responsible for my daughter's death, he may be dangerous and I suggest you proceed with caution. Set some ground rules and stay alert."

Emily nodded, agreeing that Chester's advice was sound, and promising to take precautions.

By the time they had finished their meal and he had walked her back to the shop and her car, Emily was already making plans for their next visit, suggesting that he come out to the cottage for lunch on the weekend so that he might see what she had done with the place and retrieve the items belonging to Sarah that she had set aside.

Chapter 17

Philip stared absently out the large window in his office at the growing number of sailboats littering the harbor. Though it had only been three days since he had posted the letter to Emily, her complete lack of response plagued his every thought, making it difficult to concentrate on anything else. The presentation of the marketing plan for the boat show was a mere two days away and he should be focused on his team and the progress or lack thereof rather than worrying over something he had no control over. Still, it was possible her lack of response was due to her thoughtful consideration of his request, and so; he continued to hope that she would allow him the access he desired.

Turning his attention to the charts ever present on the antique drafting table in the corner of his office, Philip ran his index finger over the passage he had long ago charted in red ink. Stopping as always in the familiar cove marked with a large X, he tapped his finger on the spot as his mind drifted to the past.

He had been ever so angry when Katherine had told him of her plans to give the property over to her sister Sarah. How could she be so thoughtless when she knew how important it was to him? The smirk on her face had sealed her fate and yet he would never stop regretting having taken the bait. Why did she find it necessary to toy with him that way? Was it that she was incapable of empathy or did she truly hate him? Acting on pure emotion he had allowed her to taunt him to the point he had little control over his actions. He should have sought out her sister and reasoned with her. She certainly had no idea that the gift had been Katherine's way of punishing him. If he had thought about things more rationally, he was certain now that Sarah would have convinced her sister to allow him the luxury of indulging him in his quest. Instead, he had permitted his emotions to get the best of him and acted without thought of the consequences.

Philip would never forgive himself for his involvement in her death and punished himself every day by living the life he had been shackled to when she was still alive. He regretted that his actions had caused his son so much pain though he often convinced himself that Sarah was a much better mother than Katherine would have ever been. Though he had kept a respectful distance from his sister-in-law for propriety sake, he had often fantasized about what his life would have been like had he met her rather than Katherine first. Like him, Sarah was a free spirit and enjoyed living life outside what was considered the social norm. Katherine had a regal beauty about her, a look only found in one that had lived a life of indulgence. Her porcelain skin and delicate features indicated she had never worked a hard day's labor and painted her as a fragile flower, though she clearly used the deception to her advantage. Still, Sarah was beautiful in her own right; hers was a beauty more natural and earthy. Her tanned skin and rough hands told a story of one who was fond of the outdoors, who enjoyed working with her hands and wasn't afraid to get dirty. Yes, Sarah was clearly more his match than Katherine in every way.

Perhaps his fondness of Sarah had not gone unnoticed by Katherine. Was it possible that her decision to give the property to her sister was her way of punishing him for his unfaithful fantasies? Was he that transparent about his feelings when they were in Sarah's company? Maybe, his eyes had given him away as they roamed over her taunt body or as they shared stories of their adventures sailing the Atlantic.

Moving over to the bar, Philip poured himself a generous glass of bourbon before returning to the comfort of his desk chair. As he sipped the liquor allowing it to warm his throat and belly, Philip recalled one evening in particular that had nearly been his undoing.

Katherine had invited a half dozen friends as well as her sister to the cottage for a mid-summer clambake, which of course was catered. She had hired a small serving staff as well as a bartender as she normally did so that she might mingle and enjoy the evening with her guests. As the evening wore on and she and her friends had indulged heavily on the alcohol, they began to retire to the cottage where they assembled in the living room to share stories from the past. Philip and Sarah were the last to remain at the fire pit, conversing easily while the caterers and bartender broke down their equipment and made their way back to their trucks.

Preoccupied with Sarah's story about a recent trip she had taken to the Caribbean, Philip had been unaware that the staff had departed and that the cottage had long ago grown quiet. Standing to stretch his back, Philip had suggested that they take a walk along the beach before retiring to the cottage for the night and Sarah had agreed, suddenly acknowledging that the hours had slipped away without her notice. Oblivious to the amount of liquor she had consumed, Sarah stood too quickly and nearly toppled into the fire before Philip grabbed her and pulled her back.

Shocked by their sudden closeness, they had stood motionless, both aware of the electricity connecting them to each other, yet neither of them willing to break it. They had held on to each other's arms, simply looking into each other's eyes for what seemed like an eternity and were about to lean in for a kiss when the banging of the screen door broke the spell and they stepped back to see Katherine standing on the porch with her arms folded over her chest in obvious disapproval.

Nervously laughing, Sarah had explained to Katherine that if it weren't for her husband, she would surely be burning alive. Unaffected by Philips bravery, Katherine had simply shook her head, straightened her back and returned to the cottage. After a moment of uncomfortable realization at what they had nearly done, both Philip and Sarah said goodnight and he returned to the cottage while she returned to the chase lounge next to the fire to sleep off the alcohol and the memory of Philip's touch.

After that, though she never made mention of the incident, Katherine excluded Sarah from future events, perhaps hoping she had been mistaken about what appeared so clearly as an indiscretion. Now though, Philip had to wonder if Katherine had held onto the image of her sister and her husband, on the verge of embrace and plotted revenge, as she was so apt to do. Katherine was never one to be obvious when it came to settling scores. For her, it was a work of art requiring much thought and consideration. Philip had seen her work first hand on more than one occasion and it still made him shiver to think of the lengths she was willing to go to in order to seek retribution.

Refilling his glass from the crystal decanter before returning to his desk, Philip recalled one victim, much like himself, that was still paying the price today for his unfortunate run-in with Katherine.

While shopping for jewelry for an upcoming gala, Katherine had fallen in love with an antique ring. Sprinkled with rubies and diamonds surrounded by intricate gold detail, the piece was both breathtaking and understated at the same time. Pointing out the piece to the jeweler, she was furious when he advised her that the item had just been purchased over the phone and he had unfortunately not had time to retrieve it from the case. Suggesting several alternative pieces with similar qualities, the jeweler attempted to satisfy Katherine to no avail. Begging him to call the buyer and offer him generous compensation for allowing her to have the piece, the jeweler had reluctantly agreed, retrieving the man's number and name from an index file behind the counter.

The buyer was not to be swayed and refused to speak with Katherine, explaining to the jeweler that he was purchasing the ring for a woman he intended to propose to and who had shown interest in the piece. Though Katherine had stood firm long after the call had ended, attempting to convince the jeweler that she was a regular customer and should receive more consideration than a man who was clearly so disassociated with the establishment as not to even personally retrieve the ring but rather order it up by telephone, her argument fell on deaf ears. Eventually another patron entered the shop and the jeweler was preoccupied long enough for Katherine to jot down the information on the card without being seen.

There were no limits to the length Katherine would go to get what she wanted and she quickly hired a private investigator to find out the identity of the woman the gentleman was to propose to. Obtaining her name along with the location of the gym in which the woman worked out, Katherine quickly got to work, the gala being only a week away. After watching her from afar for a couple of days, Katherine approached the woman and introduced herself as an acquaintance of her boyfriend, stating that she had thought the woman looked familiar and only now realized where she knew her from. Having no reason to doubt her, the woman spoke freely about herself and her boyfriend. By the fourth day, having set the scene suggesting that she was to be dining that evening with mutual friends, Katherine portrayed a woman deeply distracted and unable to focus on trivial conversation. When the woman asked Katherine what was bothering her, she suggested that they have a drink after their workout, implying she had something weighing on her mind. After plying the woman with several drinks, Katherine explained that one of their mutual friends, whom she was not at liberty to identify, had let it slip that the woman's boyfriend was having an affair.

Though the woman was reluctant to accept the information at face value, she did admit that he had seemed rather distracted of late. Philip's jaw tightened even now recalling how pleased Katherine had been with herself at having planted the seed. She had actually laughed at the fact that his anxiety over popping the question had been interpreted as infidelity. Two days later, hours before the gala was set to begin, the jeweler had phoned her advising her that the ring she had shown interest in had been returned by the buyer and was now available for purchase. Katherine had sent Philip to retrieve the ring while she prepared for the evening.

Later Philip had heard that the man had attempted to commit suicide by taking several pills, which although not lethal; had left him brain-dead and forced to live the remainder of his life attached to machines in a vegetative state. It still sickened him to think about Katherine's response to the news. He had expected her to feel terrible about what she had done and try to make amends by reaching out to the woman she had betrayed. Instead, she had shrugged it off as collateral damage and cut the woman out of her life without so much as a thought of the lives she had destroyed.

So many times he had thought about leaving Katherine, but knowing what she was capable of terrified him. He was ashamed of his role in keeping her secrets and hoped that by distancing himself from his son, he would somehow be able to shield him from the truth about who his mother really was. He had sacrificed his relationship with his only child, as well as what could have been a wonderful life with Sarah, all to protect those he loved.

"For what?" he muttered to himself now, "For what?"

A light tapping at his office door brought Philip out of his self-pity and he turned his chair to acknowledge his secretary and motion her to enter the room.

"Yes..." he responded, setting his empty glass on his desk.

"There's an Emily Gaudet here to see you...she doesn't have an appointment." She whispered, approaching the front of his desk.

"Emily...yes, of course...please show her in." He stuttered, while standing to straighten his suit and tie. "And bring us some coffee, if you would."

"Of course, Sir." She said, while scurrying across the office and gesturing to Emily, who was standing outside the door, to come in.

Philip waited while his secretary closed the door before coming around his desk to greet his unexpected guest.

"Emily...this is such a pleasant surprise. Do come and sit, I've asked my secretary to bring us some coffee." He said while gesturing her toward a small seating area consisting of two high-back chairs separated by a small round table.

"I hope I'm not intruding Philip, but I thought a personal visit rather than a phone call was in order." Her face flushed as she nervously fidgeted with her purse strap.

"Not at all, I'm glad you came." Philip smiled warmly while he waited for his secretary to pour their coffee and retreat once again to the outer office. "I hope you didn't find my note too impersonal, I just didn't want to upset you by another intrusion...I thought this way the best." Now it was he who was flustered.

"I appreciate your honesty, Philip. And of course you're welcome to search for Katherine's ring. But there's another reason for my visit." Emily paused, taking a sip of her coffee before continuing.

"I have been cleaning out some of the closets and I found a box of items that have piqued my curiosity."

"Oh?" Philip questioned, intrigued by her revelation, "What is it?"

"Well the box was filled with several old items that seemed to have either washed ashore or been located on the property by Sarah. They appear to be quite old, perhaps something from an old shipwreck and I was wondering if you knew of any ships that may have gone down in the area. I know that you are quite knowledgeable in all things relating to boating and thought maybe you might know the history of the cove."

Again Emily stopped and took a sip of her coffee allowing Philip a chance to respond.

Philip took a steadying breath before speaking. "That's very interesting. Do you still have the items in your possession?"

"Yes, I was going to donate them to the local museum, but I would like to have more information regarding their historical significance before I do that. That's why I was hoping you could help me out."

"Is it possible that Sarah might have investigated the items herself? Did you come across any research she might have done?" Philip asked eagerly, hoping there was no one else involved.

"The only thing I came across was a book on nautical antiques. Perhaps she was merely interested in identifying the items. Chase often spoke about treasure hunts they went on, but according to him, it was all for fun and he believed she was hiding the items for him to find. He had witnessed her hiding things one night when she thought he was asleep but he had never let on that he knew."

"Hmmm..." Philip scratched his head while he considered how he should respond. "It's possible of course that there might be remnants from a shipwreck or two, though I'm not aware of anything specific. Would it be possible for me to look at the items? Perhaps I can find some indication of a time period that might identify their origin."

"That would be wonderful. Like I said, I would love to donate the items if they hold historical significance. Perhaps you could stop by this weekend, Chester will be joining me for lunch, it might be nice to involve him as well."

"No!" Philip insisted before getting hold of his emotions and hoping Emily wasn't regretting her decision to allow him into her life. "I'm sorry...I apologize, I didn't mean to...look...Emily, there's something you need to know. Chester and I...well...we don't exactly see eye to eye. Even though he allows me to remain in his employ, he has never been fond of me. I don't come from the sort of family or money that he considered worthy of his daughter's hand in marriage. Even though I have tried to prove myself valuable to his business, he will never consider me his equal, nor will he ever forgive me for his daughter's death. I'm sure it's no secret to you that he believes me to be somehow responsible for Katherine's demise."

Emily silently nodded her head.

"I think it would be best if you don't tell him that I am assisting you in this area. He would only attempt to undo our relationship. It would probably be wiser if we met when he wasn't around. Let me do a little research, I know a few local historians that might be able to provide me with some background on the cove as well as literature pertaining to the artifacts. Once I have what I need, I'll call you."

"Okay," Emily responded, "You're probably right. The last thing I want is tension between you two." Rising from the chair she extended her hand to Philip. "I look forward to hearing from you Philip."

As he watched her exit his office and disappear from sight, Philip took a deep breath. He had come way too far to blow this opportunity now. He had better get a grip on his emotions before they were his undoing.

Chapter 18

Emily returned to her shop to find two unexpected patrons secretly conversing with her part-time assistant. The scandalous whispers of Cara and the intoxicating laughter of Vicky told her that she was most certainly the topic of discussion.

"Don't believe a word they say." Emily instructed her assistant, approaching the trio and pointing an accusing finger at her friends. "Their stories hold little to no truth whatsoever and would never hold up in court."

Greeting their friend with hugs, while feigning ignorance to her accusations, the women winked at her assistant, who laughed before returning to the shelves to resume her work.

"So what brings the two of you out here in the middle of the day other than the opportunity to regale my help with fictitious tales of my indiscretions?" Emily asked, crossing her arms over her chest.

"We have come to rescue you from your workplace prison and take you out to lunch." Cara announced, pulling at her arms and shaking them out.

"And..." Vicky added, smiling ear-to-ear. "we have loads of gossip."

"Well...in that case...what are we waiting for?" After apologizing to her assistant for once again leaving her to man the shop, Emily and her friends departed in search of provisions.

"Okay..." Emily said after they had placed their orders and the waitress had left their table. "What's so important that you drove all the way out here in the middle of the day to tell me? Not that I'm not glad that you did, of course."

"Of course." Cara chimed in, winking at Vicky who was so eager to reveal her news she nearly spilled her water down the front of her shirt. "Tell her, Vicky." Cara encouraged.

Emily looked to Vicky who under closer scrutiny did appear to be holding back news of great importance.

"I'm pregnant!" Vicky blurted out, placing her hand on her belly.

"Oh, Vicky...that's wonderful." Emily said, rising from her chair and rushing over to her friend to hug her. "You and Aiden must be so happy."

The remainder of the lunch hour was spent with Cara and Emily suggesting names and planning baby showers while this allowed Vicky little time to respond to their ideas. Eventually, after trying repeatedly to interrupt the two, Vicky sat back and watched with amusement as her best friends discussed everything from nursery themes to dance studios and little league teams depending on the sex of the child. By the time the check arrived, Vicky was certain they had everything planned all the way up to her child's options for college. Before they returned to the bookstore, Emily insisted that they stop at a small toy store where she might purchase the baby his or her first teddy bear.

As she hugged her friends goodbye and watched as they disappeared out of sight, Emily felt a bittersweet tug at her heart. She was so happy for her friend and what the future held for her and yet she couldn't help but think of what she had lost out on when Chase had died. Shaking off the self-pity that was about to ruin what was otherwise a wonderful day, Emily returned to her little office in the back of the shop to go over her books and focus on anything else but herself.

Chapter 19

With Saturday's forecast being less than ideal for a picnic on the beach, Chester had phoned Emily and suggested she join him at his estate. Relieved that she wouldn't have to spend her Friday night cleaning the cottage and preparing a meal for the following day, Emily eagerly accepted the invitation.

Dressed in a crisp pair of trousers and a button-down dress shirt, which was about as casual as Chester ever allowed himself to be, he sat on the elegant bench at the foot of his bed to tie his shoes. As he fumbled with the laces he cursed himself for allowing his last meeting with Emily to unsettle him so. The mere mention of Philip's name had sent him spiraling into an unhealthy mental state he had little hope of escaping without consequences he was unwilling to face.

Apparently Philip wasn't done searching for the treasure that was Chester's to find. Chester had been researching the missing cache long before Philip was able to walk, using his vast resources to acquire experts to chart the passage of the ships, long ago lost at sea. He had hired a local historian to translate a number of ships' manifests dating back to the 1600's in order that he might determine their route of passage. How could he have known that his daughter would end up marrying the historian's best friend? When he had spotted him across the room at the rehearsal dinner, he had assumed the man had tracked him down to bring him news of a discovery that would finally pay off, but when he approached him, Philip had stepped in to introduce the men, unaware of their partnership.

Of course it hadn't taken Philip long to convince his friend to divulge the nature of their relationship and once he knew there was no undoing the damage. Philip had come to Chester, asking to be included, promoting himself as an expert on all things nautical. For a brief moment, he had actually considered an alliance, but then he received word that Philip had talked Katherine into purchasing the property he himself had intended to buy, any possible collaboration he had considered with Philip was no longer an option. And so, Chester, who was never one to give in, reconciled to keep his distance while maintaining a watchful eye on both Philip and the property. If there were treasure to be found, he would have no problem convincing a judge, many of whom held memberships at the same golf club as he; that Philip had obtained the information leading to its discovery illegally, having stolen it from Chester, and he would be forced to relinquish any profits to him.

Keeping Philip in his employ even after Katherine's death had been difficult, but necessary. Chester had even warned Sarah against allowing Philip access to the property, claiming his presence there would be considered inappropriate by society. Though Sarah had argued in Philip's favor, perhaps a little too strongly, she had ultimately agreed to limit his visits to social functions that included the entire family. His plan had worked and though he was aware that Philip had continued his research as he himself had done, the limited access had prevented the late comer from confirming any of his leads.

Sarah, on the other hand; had mentioned to Chester and his wife that she had found various objects scattered along the shore, peeking out of the sand after strong storms, that appeared to be very old and possibly of great historical significance. Chester had purchased her a book regarding nautical antiques and encouraged her to adopt a hobby of searching for treasure, something that thrilled and excited the adventurous child within her.

And so, she had spent every summer, while entertaining Chase, digging for buried treasure and cataloging her finds in a leather-bond journal Chester had presented her with as a sign of his approval.

Happy to have finally made her father proud after years of his unspoken disappointment with her life choices, Sarah had eagerly indulged in this new obsession, making it both fun and exciting for her and her nephew. Though many of the items they found held little if any value, the digs themselves held endless possibilities. Sarah's love for her nephew and her desire to relieve him of the pain of losing a mother so young, continued to fuel her commitment, even when it seemed there was nothing left to search for. She only stopped when Chase went off to college and seemed to have outgrown such childish games. She had tucked away the few items that they had found, satisfied that they had served their purpose in distracting both Chase and herself while they licked their wounds.

Though Chester had tried to reignite her passion for adventure, Sarah had moved on to painting and so he had backed off, determined to continue the search on his own. Limiting his searches to off-shore excavation, Chester hired a team of divers to map the ocean floor just outside the cove to determine whether or not there were any signs of wreckage. Chester hoped to find large pieces of vessels that may have settled and remained in the area occasionally depositing smaller objects into the shallow cove and ultimately onto the beach. The work had been slow and tedious as the divers searched the area grid by grid. Due to the often-unfriendly New England weather, the divers were only able to work four months out of the year before returning to their homes in the Caribbean. He had chosen not to draw on local exploration services for fear that they might get greedy and feed him false information, but instead had traveled to the Caribbean in search of individuals skilled in diving whom he could pay generously to secure their commitment to him and his quest.

For three years, the men had come back, each year getting closer and closer to their goal. The first season, of course had been spent merely mapping the area and sectioning it into grids for future exploration. The second season had been more exciting as the men had come upon the remnants of a schooner dating back to the late 1800s. The vessel's wooden hull remained nearly perfectly intact however; Chester had been disappointed to hear that her cargo was merely cottonseed oil. Because the divers had spent nearly the entire season in the area, no other progress had been made.

The following year the crew had located the wreckage of a Spanish brig whose wooden hull had been stuck to a reef for so long it had become a part of it. Fearful that another season would be wasted, Chester instructed the divers to simply mark the spot and continue their exploration of the remainder of the region. His decision, as it turned out was a wise one; as only a month later they encountered a bark freighter. Unfortunately, its cargo had turned out to be lime, packed in wooden barrels and by the time they had completed their excavation of the site, the season was all but over and the men returned to their homeland.

By this point, Chester was greatly discouraged and wondered if he was on a fool's errand. Perhaps his research had been flawed. How much money was he willing to risk in search of a treasure he might never find?

A soft knock at his bedroom door interrupted his reverie and Chester looked up to see his housekeeper standing in the doorway.

"Sir…your guest has arrived. She's waiting for you in the library."

"Thank you," Chester responded, standing up and checking his reflection in the full-length mirror before leaving the room.

His bones creaked as he walked; reminding him that he wasn't as young as he used to be. As he slowly made his way to the main floor of his home by way of the grand staircase, his knees ached and he held onto the rail for support. He found Emily seated in one of the leather wingback chairs that looked out to the sprawling lawn. As he approached, she stood greeting him with a warm smile.

"It's so nice to see you again...thank you so much for inviting me." She said as she leaned in to kiss his cheek.

"It's my pleasure, dear, do sit down." He requested, motioning her back to her chair while he seated himself in its mate. "It's unfortunate that the weather didn't cooperate, but there's still enough of the summer left to try again."

"Yes of course." Emily responded suddenly wondering what they would find to talk about now that they didn't have the calming affects of the sea to distract their thoughts. Looking out the window at the darkening skies, Emily added, "Have you ever considered selling this place and finding something a bit smaller? It's such a large home for one person."

"There was a time after my wife passed on that I gave it some thought, but I find it helps me stay connected to her, as well as my children and I'm afraid if I leave it behind those memories will fade. Foolish I know...but each room in this house brings back memories of one thing or another." Chester looked around the library, seemly lost in the past.

"Actually, I understand exactly what you mean. It's the reason I decided to move to the cottage. Even though Chase and I never spent any time there together, all the stories he told me of his summers there make me feel as though I shared those experiences with him. When I see the bed that he slept in as a child, I remember him describing how he would pull the sheet over his head and use a flashlight to read when he was supposed to be sleeping. When I see the crack in the bathroom window, it reminds of the time he told me about nearly getting caught sneaking back in the cottage through the window after doing some night fishing when his jacket got snagged on the stick that held the window open and it came crashing down. He said Sarah came rushing in and he barely had time to unzip his fly and pretend to be peeing. Apparently she was so embarrassed that she immediately closed the door giving him time to toss his jacket out the window to collect the next day. He told her that his elbow must have dislodged the stick." Emily explained, laughing at her late fiancé's antics.

"That boy had quite the imagination." Chester agreed, "I remember one Christmas when he was probably eight or nine. Chase was obsessed with pirates that year and my wife had given him a toy box that looked like a treasure chest along with a costume that included an eye patch and pirate hat. He wore them all through the day running from room to room and forcing each of us to part with a coin or two. He even wore the patch for Christmas dinner though my wife did insist he remove his hat at the table. When it was time for him to leave with his father I was going to carry the toy box out to the car, but the thing was so weighted down I couldn't lift it. We opened it up and found a silver tea set from the dining room, my wives jewelry box, complete with jewelry as well as a couple of brass candle holders. Apparently when no one was looking he had helped himself to a fair amount of treasure." Chester roared with laughter.

Emily joined in and by the time the housekeeper arrived with a tray of sandwiches and ice tea, the two of them were practically rolling on the floor. Giving them a disapproving shake of her head, she set the tray down, perhaps a bit too forcefully, before turning on her heels and leaving the room without so much as a word. Her disapproval only made them laugh harder and before she knew it, Emily had tears running down her face.

Holding her stomach, Emily hiccupped "Oh, my stomach...I have to stop...oh that sounds just like something he would do." Dabbing her eyes with a napkin she grabbed from the tray she took several steadying breaths to calm herself.

"I was not surprised he became a writer." Chester added, "It was his way of living out the adventures he was too old to get away with as an adult. I find the main characters in his novels are a great deal like Chase himself."

As the rain continued to fall, hard and steady, Chester and Emily ate their lunch and talked about everything from the state of the economy to its effect on the housing market. At least twice during the afternoon, Emily nearly confided in Chester regarding her conversation with Philip only to think better of it when he spoke unkindly of his son-in-law. Perhaps Philip was right, it didn't seem likely that Chester would approve of her allowing him access to the property and so she was better off not mentioning it.

By the time they said their goodbyes and she drove toward home, Emily was certain she had made the right choice. Her thoughts drifted to Chase as she realized for the first time how difficult it must have been for him growing up in a family so obviously divided. She wondered if he too had felt the tension amongst his closest relatives. Perhaps it was only because she was an outsider that she was so aware of their animosity toward each other. It seemed unlikely that either Chester or Philip would have voiced their hatred for each other to the only living relative that connected them. Still, she thought, one needn't speak the words to see the hatred they so clearly showed in their facial expressions when the other was discussed.

No, she decided as she pulled into her driveway and turned off the car, she wouldn't put herself in a situation where she had to referee the two; she would keep her relationship with each of them separate and avoid conflict at all costs. That's what Chase would have wanted. Although he was not particularly close with either one of them, it would have made him happy to know that she was at least trying to develop some sort of relationship with them both.

Chapter 20

Reaching in his pocket, Riley pulled out a crumpled twenty-dollar bill, the last bill he had. He had been stupid to think he could pass through Atlantic City and merely gamble a couple hundred. It had only taken him a few days to blow through all the money he had, leaving him just enough to buy a bus ticket back to Rhode Island and a cab ride to the club. Now, as he straightened out the bill and handed it to the cabbie, he regretted having ever gotten off the bus. He should have known better. He should have stuck with his original plan and continued on to Florida.

As he stepped out of the cab with the eight dollars the cabbie had handed back to him, he stood outside the club watching as the taxi drove away. Pulling a cigarette out of his dwindling pack, he lit the end and stared at the dilapidated building. At least he hadn't shot his mouth off to his drinking buddies. Failure was one thing, but he still had his pride. For all they knew, he had just decided to take a break from drinking or hooked up with some whore; better that than listen to them confirm what he already knew – that he was a loser that would never know a life any better than this.

Tossing the butt to the ground and grinding it out under his heel, Riley took a deep breath and opened the door, inhaling the smoke and stale beer that never seemed to dissipate from the small space. One of his friends motioned for him to join him at the bar and an hour later it was as though he had never left.

With only two-dollars left to his name, Riley was one of the last to leave the bar. He had sipped his beer slowly, making it last while he half listened to his friend who filled him in on what he had missed while he was away. As he walked in the direction of his old apartment, he hoped that his roommate hadn't noticed his absence and he still had a place to live. He needed to get some sleep before he returned to the docks and tried to explain why he hadn't shown up to work in nearly a week.

Luckily, it seemed he wasn't the only one to disappear for a few days, he thought, looking around the small apartment where it appeared nothing had changed. The dirty clothes he had shed before heading to the station were still where he left them. Not that he expected his roommate to pick up after him. Tossing his backpack on the floor, Riley headed for the bathroom, eager to wash the filth of two days living between busses and bars. As he stood in the shower letting the steam and hot water wash away his fatigue, his head throbbed with the realization of what he had done.

What if the boss wouldn't take him back? What if he couldn't make rent? What if he couldn't scrape up enough money for beer and cigarettes? With panic setting in, he slammed his fist into the shower wall, jumping back as a loosened tile hit the tub floor.

"Damn it!" He grunted, rubbing his swollen knuckles.

After drowning his sorrows in a bottle of Jack Daniels he found in the back of the refrigerator, Riley had eventually fallen into a fitful sleep, only to be awakened by his roommate with a kick to the side.

"Hey…where ya been? You coming to work?" It wasn't so much a question as it was a half-hearted statement. Quite frankly, he didn't much care where the guy had been or whether he worked, so long as he paid his share of the rent.

Riley rubbed his eyes, trying to remember where he was and how he had gotten there. Dragging himself up to a sitting position and then testing his standing ability while hanging onto a nearby table, Riley merely grunted in response. He was still half asleep and wasn't really listening anyhow. Somehow managing to make it to the bathroom before he puked up whatever remained in his stomach from the day before, he washed his face and brushed his teeth before stumbling out the door, hopeful that he still had a job.

Though he was still furious with Riley for bailing on him, his boss agreed to take him back, though not before telling him what a loser he was and how pathetic his life was, like he didn't already know. For a good twenty minutes, in front of all the other guys, his boss lit into him, telling the other men that Riley was an example of what happens to a person when they allow alcohol to take priority in their life. Warning him that he was on probation and that one more screw up would be the end of him, his boss turned on his heels confident that at the very least he had humiliated the man.

As the day dragged on and he grew hungry, Riley realized he had to get some quick money just to make it through until payday. Perhaps he could talk *the man* into giving him a little work if he could figure out where to find him. Because he had always sought him out and never given him a name, it was going to be difficult if not impossible to find the guy. The only thing he did have was a phone number, but it probably wasn't smart to call the guy. He could return to the cottage and see if he could steal something, but he wasn't sure he was willing to risk going to jail. In the end, he decided he didn't really have a choice and dialed the number, hoping it hadn't been disconnected now that their business was done.

Chapter 21

Chester ran the palm of his hand over the aging leather of a ship's log dating back nearly two hundred years. The name of the vessel was all but worn away due to the harsh conditions it endured those many years ago as told within its pages. Though the writing was difficult to read, not only because of the faded ink, but also due to the shaky hand of its author, the log told a story all the same. Each page held the date along with the latitude, longitude, wind direction, sky condition and their speed as indicated by the chip log. Each time the vessel arrived at a port, a notation was made of the ship's location as well as their reason for the stop.

According to the log, this ship worked in a triangular pattern. Beginning on the coast of Africa, the ship was loaded with several dozen slaves as well as several hundred pounds of pepper. The ship would then sail to Barbados where they would acquire molasses and several barrels of sugar before continuing on to Newport. In Newport, the cargo would be unloaded and the ship would then be loaded with several thousand gallons of rum before returning again to Africa. And so it went, each page telling a piece of the story. Several notations were made throughout the log pertaining to the loss of life. Whether it be crew, swept into the ocean by the sea's unforgiving waves or a slave that developed a cough and was tossed overboard as not to infect those remaining.

One thing was certain; life on a ship was not an easy one. Yet despite these hardships, it would seem that the ship's captain could not imagine any other way of life, noting several times that while his ship sat in port he would stand guard at her helm anxiously awaiting the crews return so that they might set sail once again. The captain admits that while his crew is off being entertained by any woman willing to oblige, he found himself longing for his love…the sea.

Placing the old log back in the glass case where he displayed it, Chester returned the case to his desk. The ship's log was just one of the many artifacts that had been retrieved from the bottom of the ocean by those in his employ, and even though its pages held little monetary value, to him it was priceless. Chester found that when he needed to remind himself why he had dedicated so much time and money to this often-fruitless endeavor, he need only read a page or two to remind himself of the sacrifices these men had made only to lose their lives to the powerful waters that carried them on their journeys.

Perhaps it was his recent visits with Emily that had caused him to reflect so intently on the years lost to the pursuit, to make him doubt the value of his own sacrifice. So much time had been lost during the course of his venture, time he would never be able to get back. He had watched from afar as his daughters had grown into women, as his wife had sought comfort in the bottle while he was focused on other things. Now, when he had buried all three of them, he stood alone, with no one to share any discovery he might eventually find. No one to share the thrill of the hunt with, no one to drown out the disappointments with.

Perhaps he should have been more tolerant of Philip, inviting him to join him in his quest. He had been so quick to mistrust him, so easily swayed by his own insecurities to consider him an ally rather than an enemy. In retrospect, they weren't all that different.

Shaking off his distraction, Chester returned to the round table in the corner of his office to look over

Philip's marketing plan for the boat show. He had to admit, as much as he disliked the man, he did have an aptitude for translating his visions. Along with the stacks of literature including contact information, excursion costs, posters and colorful business cards, Philip had included a sampling of the various promotional products he intended to give away at the show. Smaller items such as floater key chains in the shape of a boat, beverage cozies and plastic mugs embossed with the company logo were to be given away as freebies. Larger items including t-shirts, tote bags and fishing hats were earmarked for individuals who booked an excursion at the show. Philip had a talent for drawing and never failed to impress Chester each year with a different design to reflect his vision, though Chester would never acknowledge that fact.

Chester sighed, again reflecting on his inability to give credit where credit was due. Why did he find it so difficult to acknowledge Philip's work? Why did he constantly feel the need to put him down? Whether he was unwilling or unable to understand his reasoning, Chester simply shook his head.

When Philip knocked at the door, Chester merely grunted, leaving Philip to wonder whether or not he was invited in.

"Sir?" Philip questioned, "Do you have time to discuss the material I left for you?" He asked, pointing to the table's display.

"It'll do." Chester responded, flinching at his own abrasiveness.

"Did you have something different in mind?" Philip asked, disappointed in his father-in-law's unemotional response.

"No, Philip, I said it would do. You can proceed with your plan. Don't get too carried away with the volume, the show's attendance has dropped significantly in the past few years. I don't want to be left with a bunch of junk I have no use for."

"I understand." Philip said, gathering the items quickly and heading for the door.

"Oh, and, Philip," Chester called, keeping his back turned as he faced the window, "Emily mentioned you requested access to the cove to search for a ring...I do hope that you will keep your intrusions to a minimum and not overstay your welcome."

Philip felt the hair on the back of his neck stand up at the implications of Chester's statement.

"Oh course... my request has but one purpose. Once the ring has been located, I won't be bothering her any more." Philip turned to the door and left the office without giving Chester the opportunity to respond.

"One purpose indeed." Chester muttered under his breath.

Chapter 22

As the heavy rains beat against the windowpanes, Emily tossed and turned trying to relax enough to fall asleep. It was still taking some getting used to living alone and nights like this weren't exactly helping. The shutters rattled against the side of the cottage with each gust of wind and though she had latched the screen door, evidently a squall had dislodged the small eyehook that secured it and the door now banged back and forth between the storm door and the side of the house. Occasional blasts of thunder followed by blinding lightening would unnerve even the bravest of souls and Emily was certainly not one of them.

Convinced she would never get to sleep until the weather calmed, Emily got out of bed and headed for the kitchen to make herself a cup of tea. She wondered how it was that Sarah had been able to endure these elements for so many years on her own, but perhaps she had been one of those rare individuals that actually found comfort in the sounds of a violent storm. Emily envied people like that; people that had the ability to connect with nature while others would run and hide under their bed.

While she waited for the water to heat on the stove, Emily wrapped her arms around each other as she stared out the window at the crashing waves. Chase would have enjoyed this, she realized. He would have held her in his arms while she shook with fear, cradling her while he muttered soothing words and when she had fallen asleep in his arms he would have gently laid her head on her pillow and snuck out of the cottage to ride out the storm, braving the elements while he teetered carelessly on the rocks. Yes, he was truly an adventurous spirit.

One would have thought that his mother's death would have made him weary of the ocean, fearful that he too might lose his life to the unpredictable waters; but in fact it was just the opposite. Perhaps his desire to make sense of her death had enabled him to put aside his natural fears so that he might better understand the workings of the tides that had taken her from him at such a young age.

The whistle of the teakettle interrupted Emily's thoughts and she poured a cup and seated herself on the sofa in the living room where she covered her legs with an old blanket. The storm continued to blow outside reminding Emily that she was but a small and fragile entity in this large and often unforgiving world. She wondered if Sarah too had sat upon this sofa during similar storms and contemplated her own life. Had Sarah ever been in love? Had she wanted children of her own or was Chase enough for her? Though she presently couldn't imagine being with another man, Emily did hope that one day she would be strong enough to move on and have a fulfilling life. It seemed somehow disrespectful to think such thoughts even now, but perhaps someday in the future, fate would connect her with someone that she could share her life with. Chase would have wanted that for her, she was certain.

After drinking her tea and finding herself still too anxious to sleep, Emily strolled over to the bookshelves and selected a novel from Sarah's collection. *Blackbeard's Ghost* by Ben Stahl caught her attention though certainly was not conducive to calming her nerves. Even so, Emily had been meaning to read the book for some time and so, accepting the fact that she was unlikely to sleep anyway, she might as well kill two birds with one stone. Returning to the comfort of her bed, she propped up a couple of pillows and began to read.

At some point, obviously quite later, as she was nearly half way through the novel, the storm dissipated and she marked her page and placed the book on the bed stand before lying down and falling to sleep. It seemed as though her head had just hit the pillow when a persistent knock at the door awoke her from her dreams. Half asleep and confused, Emily glanced at her alarm clock; shocked to see it was after ten in the morning. Panic arose briefly before she realized that it was her day off from the shop and she was about to close her eyes again when the knocking that had awoken her resumed and reminded her of what had disturbed her sleep in the first place.

Grabbing her robe from the end of the bed and stuffing her feet into her slippers, she glanced quickly at her reflection in the mirror before shrugging her shoulders in defeat and heading for the door. As she approached the door, she could see Philip through the window and was relieved that it wasn't a stranger.

"Good morning." Philip said, and then looking confused by her appearance. "I'm sorry…did I wake you? I do have the right day, don't I?"

"Yes…yes," Emily responded, opening the door wide to allow his entry while fussing with her disheveled hair, "Apparently I overslept, I'm usually not still in bed at this hour."

Emily explained how the storm had kept her awake while she prepared coffee for the both of them. Once the coffee was ready she invited Philip to make himself comfortable while she got dressed. Quickly pulling on a pair of shorts and a t-shirt and tying her hair up, Emily returned to the kitchen where she found Philip staring out the window at the cove.

"I'm sorry. I should have offered you something to eat." Emily apologized as she opened the door to the refrigerator. "I can make you some eggs."

"I'm fine, really…if you would like to eat, I can go ahead out and you can join me when you're through." Philip suggested; eager to begin his search.

"Nope, I'm good…shall we get started?" Emily proposed, finding herself suddenly tingling with excitement over what the day might uncover.

Philip held the door open for her as they stepped out onto the porch and Emily got her first look at what the storm had washed ashore.

"I had no idea how violent the storms could be out here. I've lived in Rhode Island my whole life, but never this close to the water."

"Yes, the ocean can be quite deceptive from afar. I've been in enough hairy situations while piloting boats to know all to well to never take her lightly." Philip handed Emily a pail containing several hand tools including a gardening fork, trowel and hand cultivator along with a pair of rubber gloves. For himself, he carried a small shovel, pickaxe, fishing spear and a clamming rake.

"Shall we?" He invited, gesturing her toward the shore.

As they made their way across the beach toward the shoreline, they acknowledged the large limbs that had been deposited on the sand as well as an abundance of seashells, seaweed and jellyfish. Making their way to the rocks at the side of the property, Philip instructed Emily to use her gardening fork to brush away the debris at the base of the rocks, working her way in from the shoreline. Climbing up to the top of rocks with his fishing spear, Philip got to work, picking sediment from in between the boulders, hoping to come across anything that might lie beneath the debris.

As they worked, Philip spoke at length about his youth and his adventures on the sea. While she listened,

Emily observed his expressions change from focused and determined to thoughtful and perhaps a little sad. Realizing she had stopped digging; Philip stopped talking and looked in her direction.

"What is it?" He asked, wondering if he had said something to upset her.

Standing up from the spot she had been digging, Emily sat on a nearby rock and stretched out her legs. "It's nothing...just...it's just...Chester..." She stuttered.

Philip smiled, nodding his head in understanding.

"Let me guess. Chester warned you not to trust me. He told you to be weary of me and my intentions." Leaning against the handle of the spear, Philip awaited her response with what appeared to be interest and amusement.

"Something like that." Emily responded, blushing with embarrassment.

"Let me tell you something," Philip stated, looking Emily directly in the eyes. "The only difference between Chester and I is that I have spent my entire life longing for the past, while Chester has spent his hiding from it." Returning to the task at hand he continued to pull debris from the tip of the spear and toss it aside before returning it to the gap to pierce the next level of rubble.

"I'm not sure I understand." Emily responded, confused by his declaration.

Again Philip stopped working and approached her, sitting down on a rock directly above her.

"Like me, Chester was not born to money. In fact, our backgrounds are quite similar. I'm proud of where I came from; in fact I would give anything to return to that simple life. Chester, on the other hand, finds his meager upbringing an embarrassment and will do whatever it takes to keep his past a secret from his wealthy friends and colleagues. I actually believe that the real reason he hates me so much is that he sees a lot of himself in me and it scares him to death."

Rising back up and returning to the spot he had been focused on before the interruption, Philip left Emily to consider what he had revealed. Smiling to himself at the satisfaction it gave him to disparage Chester in any way possible, he continued his efforts knowing that he had managed to chip away at the wall of doubt his father-in-law had built up against him.

As the noon sun began to beat down on them, shining directly overhead, a flicker of light escaped from between the rocks just to the right of where Philip was working. Moving in closer, he again saw what appeared to be a reflective twinkle and set aside his spear to attempt to dislodge the rock. Calling Emily to assist him in the task they were able to push the rock with their legs and send it tumbling down to the sand below. Brushing away the sediment with his gloved hand, Philip unearthed what remained of a pewter goblet. Though the stem was severed, perhaps from being ground between the rocks, the cup itself remained intact. Instructing Emily to retrieve her trowel, Philip continued to brush away the dirt and residue in search of the cups base. Their hands moved in unison as they eagerly extracted years of debris in search of more treasure. Neither spoke as they pulled the base of the cup from the hole they had dug, simply smiling at each other in satisfaction. Emily picked up the goblet, holding it out as Philip placed the base beneath it, connecting the pieces together.

"It's beautiful." Emily exclaimed in awe. Philip simply nodded, speechless from the find.

Taking the base from Philip's hand and placing the two pieces behind them on a flat rock, Emily excitedly pulled Philip to his feet. "Let's find more."

Philip laughed at her enthusiasm finally finding his voice. "I do believe you have caught the bug." He chuckled, happy to finally have someone to share his passion.

Suggesting they loosen and dislodge the adjacent rock, they began to toss small stones onto the beach until they had cleared away all the supporting rocks, leaving the large boulder only held in place by an even larger one beneath it. Again they leaned against the higher shelf and pushed with their legs until the boulder crashed to the beach, sending them sprawling and dazed. Laughing at each other, they brushed themselves off and began clearing away the sediment.

For the next two hours they continued to work, encouraged by scattered bits of pottery as well as what could only be described as an interesting piece of twisted metal. Neither Philip nor Emily could identify the item in its present condition, but they set it aside with their other finds to mull over later. As the heat of the summer sun intensified, they slowed their pace until their thirst and hunger got the best of them and they agreed to call it quits for the day.

Before Philip left, they agreed that Emily would attempt to clean up the pieces and photograph them so that they could research their origin at a later time. Philip graciously thanked Emily for joining him in this adventure, while she insisted that it was he that deserved the thanks for a most enjoyable afternoon.

As he drove away from the cove and the little cottage, Philip couldn't help but wonder what it would have been like to share this adventure with his son. Would Chase have indulged him in his pursuit or would he have considered him a foolish romantic as Katherine had? Unfortunately, he would never know.

Chapter 23

Riley glanced at his watch for perhaps the sixth time in less than an hour, aware that every individual who walked through the doors of the building suspiciously appraised him, confident that they might need to later describe the man who was so obviously out of place in a building which housed Newport's elite businesses. Not one to cave under scrutiny, Riley returned their stares, grinning as they quickened their pace to distance themselves from him.

This was not the ideal plan, but when he tried to call *the man*, he found that the number was no longer in service. It was smart, really. After all, they had agreed their business was done. Riley was certain his return wouldn't be welcomed, but then again, it wasn't like he had a choice. On the rare occasions they had met, neither had been willing to exchange names, and so; without a way to contact him, the only hope he had was to wait in the lobby of the building of the guy he had been told to call with the message before leaving town and hope that *the man* might show up at some point. It was a long shot, he knew but he wasn't one to spit in the eye of fate and it was fate that had brought him here.

Strolling the docks after a long and exhausting shift, Riley was racking his brain trying to think of a way to track down *the man*, when he had stepped right into a big pile of dog shit. Cursing the dog, his life and everything in it, he had scrapped off what he could on the edge of the dock and looked for the nearest trash can to hopefully find a discarded napkin or some sort of paper to wipe the remainder off with. As he approached the can, which was next to a small bench facing the water, a man passed by and tossed a newspaper into the trash. Grabbing the top section, Riley tore out a page and wiped the bottom of his boot and was about to tear off another page when a name jumped off the page.

"Well, well," He muttered, recognizing the name as the guy he had been told to call. "Maybe life isn't so bad after all."

Had it not been for fate, Riley was certain he never would have recalled the name of the guy he had called, so it had to account for something. The traffic through the lobby was starting to slow down and he glanced at his watch again noting that it was nearly nine o'clock and if *the man* worked in the building he would certainly be there by now. Exhausted and hungry, he was about to call it quits for the day and head back to his apartment for some sleep when they spotted each other.

"What are you doing here? I thought you left town." *The man* whispered, grabbing his elbow and steering Riley toward a side door.

"Change of plans." Riley muttered, pulling his arm out of *the man's* grasp and standing firm. "I need some more money."

The man looked around, nervously scanning the handful of people still making their way through the lobby to their destinations. "How did you find me?" He demanded through gritted teeth.

"It's not important. What's important is that I get some quick cash." Riley extended his palm, confident the man would oblige if for no other reason than to get rid of him.

"Put your hand away for God's sake. Are you stupid! Don't think you can come here and extort money from me; I'm no idiot."

"I never said you were." Riley said calmly, "I'm more than willing to earn it."

"I no longer require your services, now I suggest you move along before I have to call for security to remove you."

"Go ahead," Riley challenged, "I'm sure they would be interested to know how it is we're acquainted."

"Don't you dare threaten me." *The man* hissed moving so close that Riley could feel the heat of his breath as he spoke.

"I wouldn't think of it." Riley responded, "By the way, how's that pretty little thing at the cottage doing? I was thinking of dropping by for a visit." Without waiting for a response to the bait, Riley turned on his heels and headed for the main doors, grinning as he heard *the man* rushing to catch up with him.

"I'll meet you at the club…seven o'clock…maybe we can work something out."

Riley stopped, turning in *the man's* direction he looked him up and down. "Maybe." He said before continuing through the door and onto the street.

He had slept the entire day, confident now that his troubles would soon be behind him; he had easily drifted off and only awoke when he heard his drunken roommate trip over something on his way into the tiny apartment. With less than an hour to shower, eat and get to the club, Riley sprang into action, grabbing the one pair of jeans that didn't stink of fish guts and a wrinkled but clean t-shirt and headed for the shower. There was no need to get to the club early; it wasn't like he had any money to drink, at least not yet.

By the time he crossed the parking lot, heading in the direction of the dark sedan parked by the dumpsters, he had already decided how much he would need to get back on track. Hopefully he hadn't burned any bridges by his vague threat toward the girl. He approached the car with caution, wondering if *the man* had it in him to end his life. Confident if he had the guts he wouldn't have needed Riley in the first place, he opened the door and got inside.

"Before you say anything," *the man* announced, "let me just say, that if you ever pull another stunt like you did today, I won't think twice about killing you. And if you so much as think about harming the girl, I will make sure your death is slow and painful. Do I make myself clear?"

"Very." Riley responded struggling to recover his footing after the unexpected proclamation.

"So...what happened to the money I just gave you?"

"I lost it at the tables...and before you say anything, I know it was stupid. I got greedy. It won't happen again. I need one more job...another five grand...then I promise you, I'll be on my way and you won't hear from me again."

"How do I know I can trust you?" *The man* asked.

"I'll give you my name, my social security number...if I go back on my word you can pin the murders of those two bodies under the cottage on me. It's all I've got; I have nothing else to offer you."

The man stared at him, considering his words. What choice did he have? On the one hand, he hadn't done anything wrong, he had merely hired the guy to do a little PI work, On the other, though; he couldn't risk something happening to Emily. It was really her he was protecting after all.

"Okay, you have a deal.... but, this is the last time."

Riley reached into his wallet and pulled out his social security card, handing it to *the man* to jot down the information before returning it to his pocket. In turn *the man* handed him five hundred dollars as a down payment along with the wallet of the dead man, which he instructed Riley to deliver to the individual he had previously phoned with another message. This time he instructed him to personally deliver the wallet to the secretary of the guy in a manila envelope with a note, which would simply read "Stay Away".

Riley got out of the car and watched as the sedan drove out of sight before stuffing all but twenty dollars in his pocket and walking into the club, slapping the bill on the bar and motioning for the bartender to pour him a drink.

Chapter 24

With the boat show only a day away Chester didn't need any distractions. Every since the recession began business had been slipping away from the industry. Companies that had stood the test of time and handed down through generations were closing their doors at a frightening rate. Gone were the days when companies rewarded their employees with fishing excursions and booze cruises. Chester reflected on the days, not so long ago when his company held contracts with local businesses whose sales staff would commission his vessels several times a year to entertain potential clients, guaranteeing his own enterprise a steady cash flow. Now, however; with Rhode Island one of the hardest hit states, all such inconsequential activity had dried up, leaving his survival dependent on tourism.

As he drove toward the office, Chester considered whether or not he too should sell the business, like so many of his peers had done. Strongly opposed to the idea only a year ago, he now seriously considered it as an option. Perhaps those that had opted to sell before going bankrupt were the smart ones. His initial disgust at their cowardice was slowly turning to understanding as he watched his own books be affected by the economy. If only he had something to fall back on, he thought, immediately envisioning the potential fortune lying on the shores of the cove. Too proud to survive the public humiliation of a bankruptcy, Chester was forced to consider every option at his disposal. It was all riding on the boat show. If Philip's marketing plan was strong enough to secure ample business for the upcoming off-season, he could simply ride it out, hopeful that business would pick up by the next summer, but if it failed, he would have to contemplate selling the business before it bleed him dry.

Perhaps he could offer the business to Philip himself as not only a way out, but as a way to stick it to the man who had been a thorn in his side since the day they had met. Smiling to himself at the satisfaction it would give him to see Philip go belly-up, forcing him to return to life of poverty, Chester pulled into the parking garage, convinced he had resolved a problem that had been weighing heavily on his mind.

Stepping out of his car and into the small elevator that would take him to his offices, Chester mentally went through his schedule for the day. Other than a staff meeting to lay out the agenda for the boat show and an afternoon conference call regarding the progress of a new vessel he had commissioned a local boat builder to build, Chester's day was free. Greeting his secretary with a warm smile and nod, he entered his office and immediately picked up the phone to call Emily.

Glancing at the antique clock on his desk, Chester realized just as the answering machine picked up that it was unlikely Emily was at the shop so early in the morning. Leaving her a message to give him a call, he set to work preparing for the day's meetings; confident his worries would soon be behind him.

The meeting pertaining to the boat show went quickly and Chester couldn't help but notice that Philip was in unusually good spirits. If he didn't know better, he would think Philip was in love, noting the spring in his step and the invariable hint of a smile on his face. Something was going on, of that he was certain; and Chester wasn't one to let an opportunity to ridicule Philip slip by.

As the staff exited the conference room leaving Chester alone with Philip, who was busy gathering up the samplings he had laid out on the table, Chester rose from his seat at the head of the table and addressed him.

"You're in a rather unusual mood today." He commented, waiting for Philip to take the bait.

"Me?" Philip asked, briefly looking at Chester before continuing the task at hand. "Just looking forward to the show, I guess. I think it's going to be a good one."

"Hmmm." Chester responded, "Is that all?"

"What else would there be?" Philip asked, stopping what he was doing and facing his father-in-law.

"That's exactly what I was wondering, Philip. Is there something I don't know?"

"Look, Chester...I'm not sure what you're hinting at, but like I said, I'm confident the show is going to bring in some new business and I'm looking forward to the event. You really shouldn't be so paranoid."

"I'm not paranoid, Philip, just cautious, I'd be a fool not to be." With that Chester stormed out of the room leaving Philip grinning to himself at his ability to rattle the old man.

By the time he returned to his office, Chester's secretary informed him that Emily had returned his call. Requesting she bring him a cup of coffee, Chester thanked his secretary and picked up the phone to call Emily. His earlier plan to ask her to lunch no longer appealed to him, his hopeful mood deflated by Philip's unusual confidence, and so he opted instead to invite her to dinner later in the week. Perhaps he would be more eager to celebrate after the boat show. If not, he could always reschedule.

Chapter 25

A light tapping at her office door interrupted Emily's concentration and she looked up from her research to see her assistant standing in front of her.

"Hey, what's up?" Emily asked, pushing back her chair to stretch her legs.

"I'm heading out to get a sandwich; would you like one?" Her assistant asked.

"Is it lunchtime already?"

"Actually," Her assistant giggled, "It's nearly two o'clock. You seemed so wrapped up in your work I didn't want to disturb you."

"Oh, I'm so sorry, you should have come in sooner, you must be starving. Go ahead; I'll watch the shop. Take your time." Emily rose from her chair, motioning for her assistant to take off.

"Can I bring you something back?"

"A salad would be great." She acknowledged, reaching into her bag and handing the girl a twenty-dollar bill. "Lunch is on me."

Seeing her out the door, Emily watched as her assistant disappeared into the crowded street. She hadn't intended to spend so much time on her research, but apparently time had slipped away without her notice.

Emily had cleaned the goblet she and Philip had unearthed as best she could, removing years of sediment. Though simple in design, the pewter wine goblet was beautifully crafted. The lack of a seam indicated the piece had not been cast from a mold. The only identifying mark was a symbol etched into the base of the cup and it was that symbol that Emily had been attempting to research throughout the morning. Having photographed the piece, Emily had scanned it and forwarded the image to a number of antique dealers in the area, hoping someone might recognize the marking and be able to date the piece. Next, she had focused on researching a shipwreck database she had come across simply typing "shipwrecks in Rhode Island" into her Google search.

Having grown up in the area, Emily was shocked by the number of recorded wrecks, having no recollection of having heard about them in any of her Rhode Island history classes throughout the years. It seemed somehow odd that her elementary school teachers hadn't latched onto the subject as she was certain it would have surely grabbed the attention of the kids, making history much more interesting.

Every since they had unearthed the piece, Emily was unable to think about anything else. The anticipation of their next search as well as the potential for uncovering something of great historical significance was overwhelming. Philip had warned her that the hobby could become addicting, but she had no idea he had been serious. With the shop barren of customers and her assistant having successfully completed her task of organizing the latest collection of books to arrive at the store, Emily paced the aisles for several minutes before giving into her new obsession and picking up the phone to call Philip.

Though he was at first disappointed that her call wasn't to inform him of the origin of the goblet and its potential value, he was delighted to hear that she was eager to resume their search. Agreeing that he would clear his schedule for a couple of days after the boat show, Emily said goodbye, glad she had taken the initiative and phoned Philip.

By the time her assistant returned with their lunch, Emily's mind was back on business and the pair discussed possible ways to draw business after the summer tourists departed. They both agreed to bringing in local authors for book signings and readings in an effort to draw business in during the off-season. Poetry reading was another suggestion that Emily agreed might bring in the sort of crowd that would return again and again.

Eager to get started, Emily returned to her office and began calling authors whose books she currently carried and was quickly able to book six writers, one for each month of the off-season. Next, she composed an ad for the Newport Daily News as well as several other small town newspapers in the area. After phoning the papers and faxing the ad for the first event in the series, Emily was satisfied she would secure enough business to make it through the long winter months.

As she straightened her desk for the day, preparing to leave, her eyes fell on the framed photo on the corner of her desk. Emily smiled at the image of her and Chase, both with red noses and rosy cheeks, warming their hands by a roaring fire. The picture had been taken at a lodge in Vermont where she and Chase along with their friends Vicky and Aiden had spent New Years Eve only a few months before he had died. Picking up the photo, Emily laughed to herself, thinking of how they had gone sledding until their toes and fingers were numb and it had begun snowing so hard they were barely able to find their way back to the lodge before sunset. After stripping off their wet clothes and changing, the four of them had returned to the common room of the lodge to warm themselves by the fire and recount their less than successful attempts to outrun the local kids on the hills. It was there that their friends and co-adventurers had taken the photo.

Choking back the lump in her throat, Emily carefully placed the photo back on her desk, fighting back the urge to give in to the tears that were welling up in her eyes. Some days she was confident that she had finally gotten to a place where she could reminisce without the fear of her emotions getting the best of her, but then moments like this crept up unexpectedly and brought her right back to the unbearable pain of Chase's death.

Determined not to allow her emotions to spoil an otherwise productive day, Emily got into her car and turned the radio on, tuning it to an upbeat song that would return her to a more positive frame of mind. The commute over the bridges was uneventful and before she knew it, she was pulling into her driveway.

After changing into a pair of comfortable sweat pants and a t-shirt, Emily thumbed through her mail, noting that the majority of it was junk. A single envelope in pale lilac drew her attention and she placed it to her nose, breathing in the familiar scent of her grandmother's perfume.

How long had it been since she had seen the woman that had held her hand through the most difficult years of her life? Moving to the couch, Emily curled up under a blanket and ran her index finger under the seal, removing the handwritten pages. Despite giving her a computer along with lessons on how to use it, her grandmother still insisted on writing her own letters. When she had first moved to Florida after Emily graduated from college, the letters had arrived like clockwork at the beginning of each month. Now though, as she had entered her 90s, Emily was lucky to receive three or four a year. Her handwriting had become more and more difficult to read and the number of pages was steadily declining. This letter was a mere two and half pages and merely contained instructions for Emily to place flowers on her parent's graves for the upcoming anniversary of their death.

Emily had only been eleven when they died tragically after an explosion in a lab where they worked. Having met in college, they had become close friends, often partnering on projects while they both worked toward their doctorate degrees. After graduating their careers took parallel paths and they soon reconnected and eventually married. Their analytical minds allowed for little in the way of imagination when it came to entertaining their daughter, who though unplanned for; they loved very much. And so, while they spent long hours working in their lab, her grandmother had raised her.

Having become a widow at an early age, her grandmother delighted in the task and raised Emily as if she were her own. Though she remembered both her parents and loved them as any child loves their parents; her grandmother was her closest ally. Because they worked such long hours during the week, it had become common for Emily to simply stay at her grandmother's house, only returning home on weekends. Her parents would stop by on their way home from work, unless it was too late, and kiss her goodnight, sometimes reading her bedtime stories and that was enough for both her and them. When they suddenly died, though Emily was sad, it had not been as difficult as it might have been if she had been closer to her parents.

The company they worked for had generously compensated the families of those lost in the accident and that compensation had paid for Emily's education at Brown. After seeing that her granddaughter successfully completed her education and had established a life with Chase, her grandmother had sold her house and moved to Florida to live out the remainder of her life.

In the beginning, Emily had visited twice a year, but as time went on and her life became more complicated, she had replaced her visits with phone calls. Then, as her grandmother began to lose her hearing making it difficult to converse on the phone, she had taken to writing her. Though Emily continued to write her once a month, her grandmother's letters were fewer and farther between and it was obvious by their content that she might be slipping into dementia. Sadly, Emily realized it was unlikely her grandmother would be around much longer.

As she ran her fingers over the shaky handwriting, Emily vowed she would make plans to visit with her grandmother, if for no other reason than to make sure she knew how much she loved her and appreciated everything she had done throughout the years before it was to late.

Chapter 26

With the boat show behind him, Philip was now free to spend more time at the cottage without the fear of Chester questioning his every move. Mindful of the approaching inclement weather, Philip had little trouble convincing Emily of their need to commit at least two days a week for their search.

Now as he drove up the driveway to the little cottage, his heart beat quicker in anticipation of what the day might bring. They couldn't have asked for a more accommodating forecast, with the prediction of clear skies, a cool breeze and a temperature of seventy-five degrees. As they walked toward the spot of their first find carrying their tools and a small cooler with bottled water, they planned their strategy of the day. Suggesting they both work from the top of the rocks, each working out from the center of the grouping in opposite directions, Philip was certain that they would be less likely to miss anything. Once the smaller rocks were tossed to the shore, leaving only the large boulders in place they retrieved their tools from the beach and returned to the top to dig through the sediment that was uncovered. Both Philip and Emily worked in silence, only occasionally calling to the other for assistance when needed. Though the weather was cooperating they were still working up a sweat and frequently had to stop for water and ultimately bathroom breaks.

By the time the sun was directly overhead, they were both exhausted and bleeding from multiple scrapes and cuts they received from sticking their hands into tight crevices. Standing up and stretching her back, Emily addressed Philip.

"Are you as hungry as I am?" She asked.

"Now that you mention it...yes." Philip admitted.

"Why don't we take a break...I prepared some sandwiches before you arrived. Let's wash up and eat."

"Sounds great." Philip agreed, holding out his hand to offer her assistance down to the beach.

As they ate their lunch, Philip mulled over their strategy. "I think we might be approaching this from the wrong angle."

"How so?" Emily asked.

"Well...originally I thought that if there was a storm that the waves would have been high and that any debris would be deposited on top of the rock shelf. But, the more I think about it...assuming that the smaller rocks were in their original positions, stabilizing the larger boulders and filling in the crevices in between them...then perhaps the debris would simply have rolled down from the rocks to the beach." Philip stopped, considering his own theory.

"But the goblet we found was near the top." Emily reminded him.

"Yes...and there may be other items that slipped through as well, but I still think that the majority of the debris would have ended up on the beach."

"If that were the case, wouldn't it have been visible and collected by whoever lived in the area at the time?"

"Not necessarily. Let's assume that the area was uninhabited at the time and there were no survivors of the wreck. Anything that was swept on shore would have either landed squarely on the shore, ultimately to be buried by the sand or against the rock base. I think if we concentrate on digging against the base of the rocks, if there is anything to be found it will be found there."

If Emily noticed that Philip no longer seemed to be searching for a missing ring, she never mentioned it and despite her initial reservations regarding Philip's motives, her own curiosity had gotten the best of her and she was now as driven as Philip was to find some relics from the past. Quickly finishing their lunch, they returned to the beach determined to keep going until they either found something or the sun set.

This time working side-by-side, Philip and Emily started at the shore and began to dig. Less than ten minutes passed before Philip hit something hard with his shovel and instructed Emily to use her gardening tools to pry the piece from the ground. First digging around the object, clearing the wet sand away, Emily hooked her trowel under the edge of the piece and loosened the metal box from its resting place. Both Philip and Emily stared at the box in awe before looking to each other and smiling with satisfaction at their latest find. In unison they moved to the nearest boulder and Emily handed the box to Philip to open. Due to the harsh conditions the piece had endured, it was difficult to ascertain what type of alloy the box was made of. Its greenish tinge indicated brass, however; the weight of the piece pointed to a less dense metal. Rotating the box in his hands, Philip noted the shift of one or more objects within its confines and he quickly suggested they bring the box inside to clean it off and attempt to open it.

As she rinsed the box under warm soapy water, bits of debris flaked off and they were able to distinguish scrollwork on top of an otherwise nondescript surface. Using a hand towel to dry off the box, she placed it on the kitchen counter and opened her silverware drawer to look for something to pry the lock with. Philip stood by, silently watching as she gently probed the keyhole, only stepping forward when the box slowly sprang open the reveal its contents. Inside the box, fused together by centuries of exposure was a mass of gold coins.

"Oh my God!" Emily shrieked, covering her mouth with one hand on top of the other.

Philip merely stared, speechless by the discovery he leaned against the kitchen counter to support the weakness he suddenly felt in his knees.

"Philip?" Emily placed her hand on his arm, drawing his attention away from the treasure. "How old do you think they are?"

"I don't know…seventeenth century maybe… it's hard to tell." Again Philip returned his attention to the box, mesmerized by its contents.

"Do you think there's more treasure out there?" Emily asked, suddenly swept up by the thrill of the discovery.

Philip looked her in the eyes, holding her gaze until she began to feel slightly uncomfortable.

"Philip? What is it?"

"I think we need to talk…it's time I was honest with you."

Taking Emily by the hand, Philip escorted her into her living room and sat down with her on the couch. Taking a deep breath to consider how he should begin, Philip mentally prepared himself for the first bit of truth he had allowed himself to utter in nearly thirty years.

Chapter 27

As he untied the boat from the tree branch it was tethered to, Riley congratulated himself for having been smart enough to follow up on his hunch and keep an eye on the cottage. His patience had been rewarded as he watched in awe while the couple searched the property and ultimately pulled something from the base of the rocks.

At first he had been confused by their actions, wondering what it was they were up to. It had appeared as though they were digging for clams and he had laughed to himself thinking they were more likely to find them in the shallow water than buried under rocks. He had watched from afar, amused by their stupidity and at the same time wondering whether he was wasting his time. He was considering just collecting his money and going on his way when they had pulled the box from the sand. Grabbing his binoculars from the floor of the dingy he focused in on the box. Though he was unable to determine what it was from so far away, the look on their faces told him it was something valuable.

Now with this latest bit of information, Riley tried to piece it all together. Obviously he had known that there had to be some reason that *the man* had been interested in the property and had wanted his interest kept a secret, but Riley had never considered the reason to be anything but a personal connection to the individuals that occupied the property. Now, however, he realized he had been naive to think *the man* would have paid him so much if it hadn't been an investment in a potential fortune. He may not be as well educated or as well off as his employer, but Riley wasn't stupid.

While he considered his next move he rowed the boat back toward Newport. The ball was in his court now. With the information he now had, he was willing to bet his life that *the man* would give him just about anything to keep his secret safe. On the other hand, though, it was possible that now that he had what he was looking for, he would no longer require Riley's services nor his silence. With that in mind, Riley considered his other options. He had to be smart about this. If he screwed up now there was no going back.

After returning the boat to the spot he had "borrowed" it from, Riley stopped by his apartment long enough to shower and change before heading for the club. He had several hours to kill before he was scheduled to meet *the man* and collect the remainder of the five grand he was promised. As he walked the short distance to the club he recalled *the man's* recent threat that he would kill him if anything happened to the girl. With that in mind, it seemed he only had one option if he wanted to acquire future funds…he needed to go to the guy that he had delivered the messages to and negotiate a fair price for everything he knew.

With his mind made up, Riley walked into the club and sat down at the bar, confident in his decision.

Chapter 28

Emily sat patiently waiting while Philip paced back in forth in front of her. After a long, uncomfortable silence he finally sat down and faced her. Taking a deep breath, Philip began by explaining how he met Katherine and her parents while working as a fishing boat pilot. It was that trip that had convinced Chester of the money to be made investing in a fleet of vessels that he could commission out and that ultimately resulted in the beginning of Excursion Charters. Besides from the charter business, Chester was also a silent partner to a handful of upscale restaurants in the Newport area.

Philip stood, once again pacing the floor as he explained how he had first become aware of the property and it's possible connection to a number of shipwrecks spanning several centuries. He explained how his best friend, a local historian had been hired by Chester to translate a couple of ships logs that he had purchased at the estate sale of a well-known oceanographer. Avoiding some of the less-flattering details regarding Chester's wife, he explained how she had confided in him regarding Chester's obsession with obtaining the property for the purpose of excavation. Philip detailed how he had convinced his friend to divulge the location of the property; something that Chester had been unwilling to do. Ultimately, he explained regrettably, it had cost his friend dearly when Chester let it be known that he couldn't be trusted and his reputation in the industry had been damaged beyond repair. Philip explained that his friend, now a part-time history professor at the University of Rhode Island as well as a consultant for the Newport Historical Society; had never forgiven him.

"Are you still in touch?" Emily asked, uncomfortable with Philip's return to silence.

"No...not really. The Historical Society has an office in the building I work out of so I see him occasionally. When we do run into each other, we exchange pleasantries, and I've attempted to apologize on several occasions, but unfortunately words can't repair the damage that was done."

Emily simply nodded her understanding.

Philip cleared his throat, but as he resumed speaking it was obvious that her question had brought up some painful memories, as there was a catch in his voice as he struggled to maintain his composure.

Philip explained how Katherine had agreed to purchase the property on the condition that he not disclose his embarrassing interest in the cove. He even went as far as to reveal that he was upset with her decision to ultimately give the property to her sister, though he didn't admit to being present the night of her death. He did, however detail some of Katherine's less than admirable qualities in her selfish pursuits, explaining how, though he certainly loved her at some point; ultimately, her true nature had tainted their relationship.

Expressing his fondness for his son, Philip went on to explain his behavior at Chase's funeral was a result of an earlier argument he had with Chester regarding his handling of the services without consulting him. It seemed that Chester had taken over the planning of the funeral without Philip's knowledge and that when he had contacted the funeral home to make arrangements; they had advised Philip that everything was already arranged, leaving him no say whatsoever in how his son would be laid to rest.

"Oh, Philip...I'm so sorry." Emily cried, suddenly overcome with emotion. "It's my fault...I was the one that contacted Chester when Chase died. I had no idea that he didn't consult you about the arrangements."

Philip returned to the couch, taking Emily's hands in his own.

"It's not your fault...don't you see? This is always the way it's been between Chester and me. I've tried to please him for years, but for Chester it's always been a competition. He's never forgiven me for buying the property out from under him. I wanted to work with him, to be partners...but he was never able to see me as anything but the middle-class youth that stole his daughter. I remind him of where he came from and it shames him. Instead of being proud of the life he has built for himself...of being proud where he came from, he has never stopped running away from his past. His taking over the funeral arrangements was just another way to pretend I wasn't a part of the family. I was so angry at the time I barely made it through the service. My anger drowned out the voices of the people that spoke that day, leaving me empty and alone to grieve in private. I refused to stand beside him, to acknowledge his presence and it infuriated him. Even though I had no intention in joining those invited back to the estate following the service, he made a point of chastising me for my behavior in front of all those in attendance, making me look like an ass."

For the next two hours Philip continued on, occasionally stopping to compose himself before resuming where he had left off. Emily sat, transfixed by the emotions pouring out from a man she previously suspected to be incapable of compassion. She now felt empathy for a man who so clearly had given up all hope of love and friendship for the possibility that he might one day find a treasure long ago lost to the sea.

When he finally stopped speaking, Philip sat back down beside her and buried his face in his hands.

Without invitation, Emily reached over and embraced the man who had barred his sole to her, silently expressing her understanding and compassion. She held him for several minutes while his shoulders heaved in unison to his sobs. Her own tears ran down her cheeks as she imagined how much it would have meant to Chase to hear the words his father had spoken. Finally, Philip took a deep breath and Emily sat back, allowing him to regain his composure.

"I apologize." Philip said, taking a handkerchief from his pocket and blowing his nose.

"Please...don't apologize. We all need a shoulder to cry on now and then. I think you were probably way overdue." Wiping her own eyes with the back of her hand, she stood up. "Would you like a cup of coffee or tea?"

Philip looked up. "No...thank you...I think I should go. It's been a long day."

Emily nodded, "I understand. Will you come back tomorrow?" She asked, hoping his embarrassment over his emotions wouldn't derail the progress they had made.

"Yes...of course. I look forward to it." Standing up and straightening his shirt, Philip walked to the door. "Thank you, Emily." He said, leaning in to kiss her on her forehead before turning and walking out the door.

Emily watched as he got in his car and drove away. Long after he had left, she stood in the open doorway, staring down the long driveway that disappeared around the bend.

Chapter 29

It had been nearly a week since the boat show and Chester anxiously paced the floor of his office while he waited for Philip to arrive with the final number of bookings they had obtained. He had granted him a week to follow up on several undecided customers, holding out hope that he would be able to charm at least a handful of companies to commit to a contract. Without these contracts, there was no hope in sustaining the business for another season.

Philip tapped lightly on the open door to announce himself before entering the large office. It was difficult to read his face as he settled himself in a chair opposite Chester's desk.

"How did we do?" Chester asked, remaining standing in front of the large window, his hands clasped behind his back.

"Not bad." Philip announced. "I was able to secure eight contracts in addition to the ten we got at the show. It's not a windfall but I'm working with the sales department to come up with an incentive package for the companies that have signed contracts. I'm thinking if they agree to book a second excursion we can offer them a private charter as a bonus, free of charge. The way I figure it is the company gets two excursions to reward their employees and the private charter can be used to entertain their best customer or customers at our expense."

Chester nodded his approval before turning to face the window. Philip waited, as Chester considered the news and gathered his thoughts.

"I remember the days when we were so busy we had to turn customers away. Now we're lucky if we book enough excursions to pay our employees and maintain our vessels."

"Things will turn around, Sir." Philip said, confident in his words.

"Perhaps we'll ride out the storm, but things will never be the way they used to be. My hearts just not in it any longer, Philip. I'm getting too old. I've been thinking of getting out of the business." Chester muttered before sitting, exhausted and defeated.

"Now's not a good time to sell, Chester, you know that. You would never get what the business is worth. We can ride this out, I know we can. We just need to hang on and be inventive. In a couple of years people will be more confident and willing to once again enjoy the luxury we can offer them."

Again, Philip waited for Chester to consider his words.

"Would you be interested in buying me out, Philip?" Chester asked, studying Philip's expression for a hint at his thoughts. When Philip didn't immediately respond, Chester continued, "It's something I've been considering for a while now. I know that you and I haven't always seen eye to eye, but I'm confident in your ability to keep the business afloat during these tough times and make it even more profitable in the long run."

"I don't know what to say, Sir…I'm not sure I have the capital necessary to buy you out, and it's not like banks are lining up to give away money these days."

Now it was Philip who stood up and walked over to the window to think.

"You don't have to give me an answer now, Philip … think about it. I'm sure we could come up with some sort of buy out that would be agreeable to the both of us. I would like to see the business stay in the family."

Chester watched closely as Philip's body language responded to the word "family", perhaps it was his imagination, but he could have sworn Philip tensed and clenched his fists as if the word he had desperately wanted to hear all these years was now excruciatingly painful to his ears.

Walking toward the office door, Philip turned to Chester.

"I'll think about it Chester…and thank you." Without another word he left the office.

Chester smiled to himself. He had rehearsed the words over and over in his mind; gone over every possible response Philip might have to his offer. It wasn't until he had added the word "family" that he was confident of Philip's reaction. Now that the seed was planted, all he had to do was wait. He had no doubt that Philip was pacing his office at this very moment, mentally calculating his assets. If he had learned anything over the years it was how much Philip needed his ego stroked. For Chester to even suggest that he was competent enough to run the business on his own had to be a huge pat on the back. That combined with the acknowledgement that they were family was certain to seal the deal.

Chapter 30

Emily dragged herself out of bed, conceding that she seemed to be making a habit of sleeping in. She had stayed up way to late and had, for the second time this week, fallen back to sleep after shutting off her alarm. Realizing she didn't have time for a shower, she washed her face and pulled her hair into a neat ponytail before returning to her bedroom to quickly dress. At least she had the good sense to select an outfit before she went to bed, as she was confident such a task would have been impossible now.

Stopping at a coffee shop on her way to work she ordered a couple of coffees as well as bagels. Once again she acknowledged how lucky she was to have such a competent assistant and decided it was time to reward her with a raise. It wouldn't be much; although the business was doing okay she wasn't exactly getting rich. Still though, it was important that she acknowledge her assistant's hard work and tolerance for her less than set schedule. Besides, given the latest treasure she and Philip had unearthed, she may soon come into some money.

After Philip had left she had spent several hours considering everything he had told her. It was heartbreaking that Chase hadn't been around to see this side of his father. A combination of empathy and regret had made it impossible for her to focus on anything else and she had found herself reliving the days following Chase's death. Desperate to rid herself of painful memories, she had dragged out the books belonging to Sarah pertaining to antiques. By the time she finally went to bed it was well past three in the morning.

When she reached the shop her assistant was already hard at work stocking shelves with the latest delivery in preparation of the upcoming book signing. Handing her a coffee and bagel, Emily announced that she was rewarding her with three percent raise in recognition of her hard work before retreating to her office. While she sifted through the pile of work on her desk, she ate her own bagel before picking up the phone to call Vicky. She had been so wrapped up in the shop and her project with Philip she had been neglecting her friends. Although both Vicky and Cara had phoned her several times to make plans, she had put them off with one excuse or another. It was time she made a commitment to them; after all, without their friendship she never would have survived the past couple of years.

First she called Vicky to see how she was feeling and whether or not she was up to a girl's weekend at this stage of her pregnancy. Vicky acknowledged that she was tired and constantly hungry but was game for whatever Emily had in mind. Though Vicky was available she informed Emily that Cara had mentioned she had plans with her latest boyfriend to go away for the weekend and so they tentatively planned to get together the following weekend assuming Cara could make it. If not, Vicky assured her; she would come alone.

Next, Emily phoned Philip's office, leaving a message with his secretary when she was advised he was in a meeting. Following through with what they had discussed, Emily found and made an appointment with a coin collector hoping that Philip would be available to go with her. With that settled she was now able to concentrate on the mounds of paperwork before her and she quickly got down to business ordering books, settling invoices and looking through the classified for upcoming estate sales where she may find more books.

She was so engrossed in her work she didn't notice Chester walk into her office and she nearly jumped out of her chair when he cleared his throat to get her attention.

"Oh dear Lord...you nearly gave me a heart attack." She said, placing her hand on her chest.

Chester chuckled before approaching her to give her a hug.

"Sorry about that...I thought I might steal you away from your work to accompany an old man to lunch."

"I see, and who might this old man be?" She said, teasingly looking around him.

"Unfortunately, it's just me." He winked, playing along.

"Well in that case...it would be my honor." She smiled, rising from her chair and grabbing her handbag. "So, what brings you here, other than my delightful company of course?" She playfully asked.

"Need there be any other reason?" Chester winked, placing her arm over his as they walked toward his favorite eatery.

"I suppose not...still though, it isn't often a handsome man steals me away from work." This time it was she who winked.

"Actually we're celebrating."

"Celebrating?" Emily asked, stopping in the middle of the sidewalk, causing more than one passerby to glare at her for upsetting the foot traffic.

Urging her on, Chester explained. "The boat show was a success...in fact Philip has secured enough bookings to get us comfortably through the winter months."

Ducking into the entry of the restaurant whose door was opened by a greeter, Emily waited until they were seated before responding.

"That's wonderful Chester. Congratulations to you and Philip." Raising her water glass she cheered his success.

"I have asked Philip to consider buying me out." He continued, watching her intently for her response. "I've been thinking about what you said and I think you're right."

"What I said?" Emily asked, confused.

"Yes, when you asked me if I ever considered selling the house…moving on…it got me to thinking. I suppose I had hung onto it selfishly hoping for grandchildren who might someday take over the business and eventually the estate when I passed on. Even though Chase was gone, I continued to cling to that notion. It wasn't until you vocalized the question that I accepted the truth." He paused, considering his own words.

As the waitress approached to take their orders, Chester raised his arm, signaling their need for more time and she silently retreated.

"I'm not a young man…it's time I get my affairs in order. I realize that Philip may not have the assets to buy me out immediately; in fact, I have asked my lawyers to come up with a few proposals that might involve a substantial down payment followed by a five year buy out. I've also contacted a realtor to work on selling the estate."

"Do you think that's wise at this time? It's not exactly a seller's market right now."

Chester nodded acknowledging her misgivings, "I know…I realize I won't get nearly what it's worth, but I would much rather be in control of my holdings than have some estate lawyer tie things up in court and ultimately sell out to the highest bidder."

"I understand." Emily said, nodding to the waitress who had timidly returned for their order.

Though the rest of their time together was filled with trivial conversation, both Chester and Emily were distracted by the heavy implications of Chester's announcement. When he finally dropped her off at the shop, Emily's mind was racing with questions. It was unlikely her off the cuff remark about the enormity of the estate had convinced Chester to sell the home and the business. Was it possible he was ill? It also seemed odd, considering his dislike for Philip that he would sell the business to him, unless perhaps he foresaw a bleak future and wanted Philip to suffer. No...she refused to believe that Chester would purposely put Philip in that position. He may not like him, but he obviously didn't hate him. If he did, he would have just fired him after Katherine died.

No...there was definitely more to this change of heart than she could possibly imagine. Perhaps Philip understood better than her.

Chapter 31

As he paced the outer office of Chester Eastwick, Riley could feel the secretary's disgust like a driving rain soaking him to his core. Every once in a while he would stop pacing long enough to glare in her direction, catching her off guard and delighting in her reddening face and shaking hands.

Once he had made the call, it had been easy enough to secure a meeting with the guy though he wasn't thrilled at the prospect of conducting business on his turf. Riley had suggested they meet at the docks, however the proposal was quickly shot down and he had no choice but to agree to a meeting in a place the guy felt most comfortable.

Three days had passed since their brief conversation and Riley was anxious to get it over with and be on his way, a much richer man. He was just about to approach the secretary to demand an audience at once, when her phone rang and she mumbled for him to follow her into the inner office. Riley had known by the guy's voice that he was an older gentleman, but seeing him for the first time gave him pause all the same. He may be a low life, but he wasn't willing to scare the man to death and by the looks of this guy, it wouldn't take much to make that happen.

Standing behind his enormous desk, Chester thanked his secretary and motioned for Riley to take a chair in front of him before returning to his own. Riley accepted, waiting for the door to click shut before addressing him.

"So I guess you're probably wondering who I am and what I know." It was a statement more than a question and he waited for Chester to acknowledge, which he did in a slight nod of his head.

Riley spoke slowly, keeping his tone even and non-threatening. Starting at the beginning nearly thirty years ago, he explained how he had first met *the man* and what he had asked him to do. He emphasized the fact that he was no criminal and that at no time had he done anything beyond that which a private investigator was apt to do. While he acknowledged that breaking and entering might not be legal, he was merely investigating and never took anything from the cottage. He further explained that at no time were any of the residents of the cottage in harm or aware of his activities. Stressing the point that he was both unwilling and unable to harm another person for any amount of money, he watched as Chester let out a breath of relief.

While Riley acknowledged that he believed Chester was responsible for the death of the two individuals under the porch, he assured him that he would take that information with him to the grave. After all, his only interest in this matter was to obtain enough money to fund a one-way trip to Florida and enough to get him set up. He was more than capable of making a living once he got there.

For his part, Chester quietly listened, giving no indication either way as to whether or not he would be willing to oblige in funding Riley's trip. After nearly an hour he finally rose from his chair and spoke.

"This man you speak of...who is he?"

"I don't know...I don't want to know. I believe he works in this building. Other than that, your guess is as good as mine."

"If I showed you some photos, I'm assuming you would be able to point him out?"

"If he was in them, yeah."

Riley waited as Chester paced back and forth in front of the window, considering all that he had learned. Finally he turned to Riley and spoke.

"I don't doubt what you've told me here today…and I won't respond to your assumptions. That being said, it would be in my best interest to work with you rather than risk the consequences of my refusal. I'll need a few hours to come up with the money. I can offer you ten thousand on the condition that you sign a note which I will compose making this payment legitimate for investigation work. I'll dig up a few photos of men I know who work in the building for you to look at. Can you come back here tonight at six o'clock?"

"That works for me." Riley agreed, rising from his chair and extending his hand to the guy.

Chester glanced at the hand before turning back to the window without accepting the gesture.

"I'll see you at six."

Riley shrugged his shoulders, what did he care if this guy didn't want to shake on it, so long as he got what he'd come for.

Chester waited as Riley walked to the door, opened it and closed it behind him. Letting out a breath of relief for having survived the encounter, he once again seated himself behind his massive desk, comforted by the protection it gave him. Reaching for the phone, Chester rang the outer office, instructing his secretary to clear his schedule for the day, announcing that he had some unexpected business to attend to. Though she questioned whether everything was okay, he assured her that it was nothing she should concern herself with and that once she had cancelled his meetings, she was free to leave for the day.

Moving to his bookcase, Chester fumbled through a stack of photos tucked inside an old book on business management, its message long ago obsolete. Amongst the stack of photos of his wife, daughters and grandson, Chester located what he was looking for. It was a photo of Katherine and Philip on their wedding day. Though his hair was now gray, Philip's face had not changed much over the years and he was certain Riley would recognize him. There was only one other likely person who might be behind the threatening messages and that was William Fitzpatrick, the historian he had hired all those years ago to assist him in his treasure hunt. It was a long shot considering that Bill was only in the building a couple days a month when he worked for the Historical Society, but still…if anyone had a bone to pick with him it was Bill.

He had only seen him a handful of times when they happened to bump into each other in the building lobby or on the elevator. On those rare occasions, he had kept his head down hoping that Chester would simply ignore him. Not one to let an opportunity pass by, Chester would always great him as though there was no bad blood between him. Perhaps he was now retaliating for making him feel so uncomfortable. No, Chester decided, if Bill had it in him to stand up for himself, he certainly would have done it before now. It was much more likely that Philip was the mastermind.

Rummaging through a stack of Rhode Island Monthly magazines, Chester looked for the May issue, recalling a photo from a fund-raising gala for the Historical Society. As he flipped through the pages his hands shook, as his mind was flooded with memories of the past. Finally locating the page, he tore the photo from the magazine, placing it on top of the photo of Philip. Perhaps he had jumped the gun in offering Philip the business. If he was the one responsible for the recent threats, did he really want him to take over the business built under his name and reputation? Was it possible Philip and William had patched things up and were working together?

Crossing his office to the small bar he poured himself a glass of bourdon, quickly downing the burning liquid and refilling his glass before moving back to his desk. His mind drifted to the past as he questioned whether he had ever been truly happy and content.

Perhaps, he thought, when he had first met and married his wife, he had been satisfied with his life. He was young and enthusiastic about the future. She had shared his dreams then, in the years before she began drinking to fill the emptiness in her life. He knew it was his fault. Not that it mattered now. He had watched from a distance as she slipped away from reality and found comfort in the bottle. He often wondered why she hadn't taken a lover or simply left him. Perhaps she had held out hope that things would change, he mused, recalling her childlike naivety. Unlike himself, his wife always saw the good in everyone. Her trust and foolish beliefs had led her down a path of pain and disappointment that she was ultimately unable to find her way out of. When she finally realized the truth, alcohol was the only way she could cope.

A knock at the door interrupted his reverie and Chester raised his eyes to see his secretary standing at the door.

"I'm sorry to bother you, Mr. Eastwick. I, um, I just wanted to let you know I have cancelled your appointments for the day. Are you certain there's nothing else you need?"

Her concerned look gave him pause and he wondered if he was making the right decision.

"Thank you...you're free to go. I'll see you tomorrow." He smiled, reassuring her, if not himself, that everything was okay.

He remained in his chair, facing the large window and sipping his bourbon slowly for nearly an hour before reaching into his desk to retrieve his bankbook.

Chapter 32

As she waited outside the coin shop for Philip to arrive, Emily mulled over her conversation with Chester. She had spent the remainder of the afternoon struggling to understand the abrupt change that had come over him. The more she thought about it, the more she convinced herself that there had to be some deeper meaning to his change of heart than he had led her to believe.

"Hey, sorry I'm late...traffic was horrendous." Philip announced, before greeting her with a quick hug. "Shall we?" He asked, waving him arm in the direction of the shop.

Emily responded with a nod of her head and a deep breath to prepare herself for what they were about to learn.

After a brief introduction, the shop owner led the pair into a back room where he offered them a seat as well as a coffee. Neither accepted the offer of a beverage, nervously agreeing they were far too anxious already at the prospect of what they might have found.

Beginning with the box of coins Emily had located in the closet, the shop owner studied each coin in silence while Philip and Emily anxiously watched and waited. Several minutes passed before he finally looked up and addressed them.

"What you have here is a collection of Spanish colonial cob coins dating back to the early 1600's."

"Are they valuable?" Philip asked.

"No, I'm afraid not. On average you can purchase similar coins in lots of perhaps twenty for approximately forty dollars on line, a bit more in coin shops."

"I see." Philip responded, obviously disappointed by the news.

The shop owner continued to give a historical account of the coin's origins holding up one coin and explaining that it was a bronze Phillip III coin while another was a Spanish 8 Maravedi silver coin and yet another was a copper coin, but seeing that the pair had lost interest he stopped talking and moved on to the second set of coins.

Philip looked over to Emily who responded by holding up her crossed fingers. Giving her a brief smile he returned his attention to the shop owner. These were the coins that they had unearthed and though Philip was certain they were likely a part of the same wreck, he continued to hope their value might be greater.

The shop owner was much quicker in identifying the second lot and both Philip and Emily were certain they would not be pleased with his findings.

"Unlike the first lot..." He began "these coins are extremely valuable. What you have here are Queen Victoria's gold sovereigns dating back to the 1870s. In my opinion, each of these coins would sell in the two thousand dollar range." Smiling, he waited for his words to sink in, noting the open mouths and wide eyes staring at him from across the table.

"Each?" Emily asked, finally finding her voice.

"Yes, each. May I ask where you acquired them?" The shop owner asked.

"We um...we inherited them from my uncle's estate. He was an avid coin collector." Philip lied.

"I see...well if you are interested in selling them I would love to make you an offer."

Philip looked over to Emily who nodded her agreement.

"How much?" Philip asked.

"Well, there are thirty coins here. I can offer you fifty thousand."

Again, Philip looked to Emily and again she nodded her approval.

"It's a deal." Philip said, offering his hand to shake on it.

Explaining that he was required to hold the coins for a period of time to make certain they weren't stolen before completely the transaction, he provided them with a contract which laid out the details of their agreement as well as providing them financial protection if the coins were stolen from his shop during the waiting period, valuing the coins at sixty thousand dollars.

A half hour later, seated opposite each other at a pub down the street from the shop, Philip offered a toast to their success.

"Here's to what is hopefully the beginning of a long and profitable partnership."

"Cheers." Emily agreed.

Philip smiled thoughtfully at Emily until his steady stare made her uncomfortable.

"What…what is it?" She asked.

"Hmm? It's nothing…it's just that I had always hoped to have a daughter, someone who would share my passion for adventure. I feel as if I have one in you. I just wish that Chase was here to share this moment with us." Philip lowered his eyes to his glass as he fidgeted with the cocktail napkin underneath it.

Emily reached across the table, placing a hand over his.

"Me too." She said, holding his hand until their eyes met and a slight smile raised the corners of his mouth.

Chapter 33

Having passed the time after his meeting with Chester Eastwick with a bottle of Jack Daniels, Riley was feeling less than steady on his feet by the time he returned to collect his money. Cautiously avoiding eye contact with the building's security officer as he made his way across the lobby to the elevators, Riley could feel the disgusted glares of Newport's elite businessmen and women as they made their way past him toward the exit. Reassuring himself that he would soon be on a bus headed south, Riley pressed the button to Chester's floor and moved back to the corner of the empty elevator for support. The pressure of the elevator rising and then settling before the doors opened was nearly his undoing and he swallowed back the bile that rose in his throat. Making his way down the hallway, he was grateful to see Chester waiting for him outside his office.

Motioning for him to take a seat, which Riley gladly accepted; Chester offered him a drink. Declining the offer, Riley settled into the chair.

"I have a couple of photos I'd like you to take a look at." Chester explained, placing the photos of Philip and William on the table in front of him. "Do either of these men look familiar?"

Riley leaned forward, steadying himself by grasping the arms of the chairs. He quickly scanned the photos.

"No." He answered before sitting back.

"Are you sure? Look carefully. They may have aged a bit since these pictures were taken."

Again Riley leaned forward and examined the photos.

"No, I've never seen these guys before …although…this guy might be the man I saw on the beach with the woman that lives at the cottage." He said, pointing to the photo of Philip.

"I can't be sure though, he was pretty far away." Riley added.

"But he's not the man that employed you?" Chester asked, frustrated.

"No, definitely not." Riley assured him. "How about that money?" He asked, suddenly growing impatient with the topic.

Chester paced the floor, ignoring Riley's request while deep in thought.

"Hey! I held up my part of the deal…where's my money?" Riley demanded, regaining his focus and standing up.

"Yes…yes, of course." Chester agreed, returning to his desk and retrieving an envelope with the cash and handing it to Riley.

Riley opened the envelope to assure himself he wasn't being taken before quickly scribbling his signature on a piece of paper Chester shoved in front of him without reading it and heading toward the door.

"It's been nice doing business with you." He said before making his way out to the hallway and the waiting elevator.

Without responding Chester sunk into the now empty chair. He had been certain that Philip was behind the threats. So certain in fact, he had only added the photo of William as an unlikely comparison. *If not them, who?* Philip he could have dealt with. Handing over the business would have been enough to keep his secret. Even William could have been handled. All he would need to do was pay him off with a donation to the historical society. His chest tightened as he struggled to come up with another face. Granted he had made a few enemies over the years through his business dealings, but no one he could think of that could be traced back over the span of three decades to the time of the unfortunate death of the cottage owners.

Rising from the chair, Chester moved to the bar where he poured himself a glass of bourbon, downing the first one before pouring a second and returning to his seat.

Rubbing his forehead, Chester thought back to the days before the encounter. William had announced that he had pinpointed the most likely location of the 1810 wreckage of a Spanish Brig that was thought to hold valuable cargo and had struck a reef of the coast of Newport and gone down. Though portions of the hull and the ships cannons had been located near the reef in the early 1960s, the ship's cargo as well as any other remains had yet to be located.

With the country focused on the Vietnam conflict, Chester used its distraction to bypass the usual channels necessary to obtain permits for excavation. When he came up empty and William recalculated his earlier measurements, he was redirected to the property now owned by Emily.

His initial intention was to make an anonymous offer to the property owners through his attorney, however William convinced him that if in fact there was treasure located on the property and he had prior knowledge of it, the owners might be able to claim; at least partial ownership and therefore it would be in his best interest to disclose his theories and offer them a deal up front. And so, with William by his side, Chester had confronted the couple and made them an offer on the property as well as a proposed 25% cut of any profit made from the discovery of artifacts.

Unfortunately, the elderly couple had refused, stating that they had no desire to tear up the beautiful coastline at the slim chance that there may be buried treasure.

Though William had been disappointed with the couple's decision, he merely suggested that Chester concentrate his focus on the area between the reef and the shore, which was likely to contain a good number of artifacts. After all, William's interest was that of a historian not of a treasure hunter for profit. Chester was not so easily dissuaded and he continued to press the couple on his own.

Beginning with gifts of expensive wines and cigars, Chester attempted to bribe the couple. At first they thanked him for the gifts however advised him that they were not likely to change their minds. After a couple of months they began to refuse his gifts and requested that he leave them in peace. Backing off for a bit, Chester concentrated on the offshore excavation, hoping that the obstruction of their view by the vessels he employed to map and explore the bottom of the ocean might entice them to change their minds. When the weather became unfavorable to his mission, he resumed his efforts in attempting to convince the owners to sell.

On the promise that he had but one final offer, the couple agreed to meet with Chester and he arrived at the cottage hopeful that his ridiculously high offer would seal a deal. Up to this point, the couple had seemed rather naive and Chester had used it to his advantage. Now, however, the couple greeted him with determination and resentment at the intrusion in their otherwise simple lives. Though they allowed him the courtesy of stating his offer, he had barely finished speaking when the old man rose from his chair, telling him that no offer, no matter how high would convince them to sell.

As he rubbed his palm across his chest, silently encouraging his heart to slow down, he wondered why.

Why now after all these years? Who from his past had held onto the knowledge of his crimes for all these years? What was different now than ten, twenty or thirty years ago? What did they want and more importantly …how would he pay?

Chapter 34

It has been nearly a week since *the man* had seen Riley slither his way through the lobby of the building that housed Excursion Charters. It had briefly crossed his mind to follow him into the elevator and confront him, but the fact that he had kept his head down avoiding eye contact with everyone around him gave him all the information he needed. It was obvious that the snake of a man had become greedy and could no longer be trusted. Parking on the opposite side of the street he had waited for Riley to exit the building, watching as he hailed a cab. Keeping his distance, he followed the cab through the busy streets and eventually onto the highway where he allowed several vehicles to separate him from the taxi until it exited, dropping its passenger at the bus station in Providence. Confident Riley was finally leaving town, at least for the present; *the man* got back on the highway and headed back to Newport.

Now that he had Chester's attention, it was time to act. Careful to blend in, he kept a watchful eye on Chester. It was evident by his nervous pace and darting eyes that he had become suspicious of everyone around him, stopping every few feet to check behind him to see if he was being followed, refusing to get on the elevator unless there were several others with him. Satisfied that he had thoroughly shaken the old man, he decided it was time to make his move.

Desperate for vengeance, he had never waivered, certain that justice would prevail in the end. In the beginning he was certain his emotions would get the best of him, that his fragile state of mind would ultimately cause him to act irrationally, but he had always teetered on the edge, never taking that extra step that would seal not only the fate of Chester, but that of himself.

Riley had been the armor that protected both Chester and himself from his sometimes-irrational thoughts, guaranteeing Chester's safety and keeping himself out of prison for a murder he was likely to commit. Choosing Riley had been easy, he was a loner, not a stupid man but certainly not savvy enough to he think beyond the present and despite his rough exterior, he wasn't willing to risk going to prison again, which was what made him so trustworthy. He knew that eventually he would have to cut him loose and quite frankly; he was surprised he was able to hang onto him for so long. If Riley was smart he had learned his lesson and would stay on the bus until he reached his destination and not look back.

As for himself, all the pieces were now in place. He had the evidence he needed to see Chester pay for his crimes, but before he went to the police, he intended to make him suffer. It was unlikely a man Chester's age would last long in prison, if he made it there at all.

The shift in Chester's usual routine had recently changed. He was leaving the office in the middle of the day, closing the office earlier than usual and word around the building was that he had recently employed a realtor to put his estate on the market. This combined with the fact that his demeanor bordered on paranoid, his own warnings and threats likely the cause; his long awaited time for revenge had finally come.

Chapter 35

Placing the large blue tarp within reaching distance of the spot they had been concentrating on for nearly a week, Emily and Philip resumed their efforts with a sand sifter Philip had crudely devised out of chicken wire and 2x4s. After several backbreaking days of shoveling and raking, it had become evident that they would require something less primitive if they were to make any progress before the cold winter months set in.

With their new method of excavation perfected, they were now able to work quickly and in three days time had covered a distance of nearly ten feet from the shoreline and approximately six feet in depth. At this rate, Philip assured Emily that they should have completed the length of the rock formation's base by the end of the week.

If what they had found to date was any indication of what else might be buried on this shore, they were likely to become very rich. Not only had they discovered several more loose coins, but they also found an intricately carved ivory smoking pipe as well as a comb made of whalebone and several bits of rope and wood coated with pine tar.

When they weren't digging and sifting through the sand, Emily was researching their various finds behind her desk at the bookstore. Using what resources she had at the various distributors she dealt with, she was able to obtain several books. Amongst the various historical accounts of shipwrecks off the coast of Rhode Island, she was able to compile a list of specific vessels believed to have gone down in the area, as well as accounts of items typically found on board these vessels. She also acquired a book regarding coin collecting and a guide on how to clean most artifacts.

Though Chester continued to press Philip for a decision regarding the buy out, Philip was careful not to make any rash decisions. Explaining to Chester that he wanted to give it more thought, he had bought himself another week, though Chester was less than pleased with his hesitancy. Although he hadn't refused the offer outright, his vague responses to Chester's questions regarding whether he was considering other options made it apparent that the business was no longer his sole source of income.

Regrettably Chester had no one to blame but himself, considering that Philip had attempted a partnership with him those many years ago when Chester himself was banking on the cove as an investment. Now, with the economy at its current state of decline and the excursion business slowly slipping away, he was likely to lose everything while Philip walked away a rich man.

As they neared a spot they had marked as a stopping point for the day, Philip leaned against the handle of his shovel with one arm while wiping his brow with the other. They had become so efficient with their work they knew approximately what time to stop digging for the day and begin refilling in the hole they had made. Using a yardstick to measure out the distance, they had determined they were able to work three feet a day in length along the rock base to a depth of six feet. Philip believed it was unlikely they would unearth anything beyond that depth. Once they had reached their goal for the day they would leave the yardstick in place so that they would know exactly where to resume their work.

Both Philip and Emily had begun working half days, giving them four to five hours of sunlight depending on the cloud cover. On rainy days or days when the wind was too strong, they spent their time cleaning the artifacts they uncovered. Though Chester had phoned Emily asking her if she was free for dinner, she had declined; stating that she was too busy with work and that once the winter arrived she would have more time for him. She hated to lie to him, but she was well aware of the pressure he was putting on Philip to make a decision regarding the buyout and didn't want to be put in a position of having to explain or defend his indecisiveness or be questioned about what he was doing with his time.

She had made time for her friends, following through with her plans to invite Cara and Vicky over for a weekend. Advising Philip of her plans, she told him he was more than welcome to continue the work on his own while she entertained her friends. Happily accepting the offer, he was surprised when she had run out on the beach to invite him to join the three of them for dinner. Philip sat back in his chair, content to listen while the three friends reminisced about his late son's exploits. Every so often, between the giggles and the stories, Emily would reach over and place her hand on his; giving it a gentle squeeze that told him she too felt the loss he was experiencing. Before Emily returned to the table with dessert, Philip quietly excused himself and joined her in the tiny kitchen.

"I think I'm going to call it a night." Philip announced. "Thank you so much for dinner."

"Are you sure you won't stay for dessert and coffee…perhaps a glass of wine?" Emily asked.

"Another time…go…enjoy your lovely friends, I'll see my way out." He said, gently kissing her check and heading to the back door.

"Will you be coming by tomorrow?" Emily asked, suddenly concerned over his thoughtful demeanor.

"No...you have fun. I'll call you on Monday." He said turning toward the door without waiting for her reply.

Though the conversation continued late into the night, Emily found herself distracted by Philip's somber mood before he departed. She had grown quite fond of the man, in fact nearly calling him "Dad" on more than one occasion. He had become somewhat of a father figure to her and the more time they spent together the closer she felt to him. Emily was certain he also felt the connection, as she watched him change from a quiet and serious man to an easygoing, carefree man with the spirit and awe of a boy. Again, she reflected with sadness on how Chase would respond to the man his father had become.

Chapter 36

Chester stood before his study window, blindly staring at the vast land surrounding his estate. The normally green grass had begun to yellow as it often did when the cold weather set in. A couple of crows circled the perimeter of the tree line that surrounded the back of the property, squawking loudly as they took turns descending upon the branches now nearly bare of their leaves. Somewhere in the distance he could hear a church bell ring, prompting his neighbor's dog into a fit of barking. With nearly three acres separating him from his nearest neighbor, it wasn't often he heard the dog. Absently he wondered if the dog had gotten loose again and was wandering the woods looking for prey.

Chester had never been an animal person, merely tolerating his late wife's Pomeranian who passed away shortly after she did. He detested the infernal yipping and shedding coat, not to mention the fact that the tiny beast was forever pissing on the floor. His neighbor owned a Golden Retriever who was constantly running away only to end up on his property, muddy and wagging her tail, eager to jump on the first person to approach it with dirty wet kisses. The thought of such an animal being someone's pet disgusted him and he had often fantasized about the dog's imminent demise.

Moving away from the window to his favorite chair, Chester unconsciously rubbed the back of his neck. For the past three nights he had barely slept, tossing and turning before eventually giving up and coming to the study for a glass of bourbon and a cigar. His lack of sleep, as well as his age, was getting the best of him and he was finding it more and more difficult to focus. He had been certain that Philip would jump at the offer to buy him out, but now, nearly a week since he had proposed it, his gut was telling him the answer would be "Thanks but no thanks."

Perhaps he should disappear for a while; take a break from everything. Lord knows it had been years since he had taken a vacation. Maybe if he left Philip in charge for a month or two he would get a feel for running the business and decide it would be stupid to pass on his offer. Yes, he decided, that was what he would do. He would have his secretary book the next flight out to St. Lucia, an island in the Caribbean he often sailed to in his younger days. It was there he had spent his honeymoon with his late wife. They had returned many times over the years and though it had undergone many transformations as it gained popularity with tourists, the lush rainforests and beautiful beaches remained unchanged.

Satisfied that he was making the right decision, Chester showered and dressed for work, leaving a note for his housekeeper advising her of his plans and asking that she pack him a couple of suitcases with the appropriate clothing.

He was just about to leave the house when there was a knock at the door. Assuming it was his neighbor looking for his runaway dog, he opened the door.

"Yes?" He asked, not recognizing *the man* standing before him.

"Chester Eastwick?" *The man* asked.

"Yes, I'm Chester Eastwick. I'm afraid you've caught me on my way out, what can I do for you?" He asked, stepping out of the house and closing the door behind him. Without pausing he continued to walk in the direction of his car, noting a dark sedan apparently belonging to the gentleman blocking him in.

"I was hoping we could talk." *The man* stated, remaining motionless on the front steps of the home.

"I'm not sure what this is about, but I'm on my way to work, I'm going to need you to move your car." Angered by the intrusion, Chester waited for *the man* to oblige.

"I'm afraid it's rather important, perhaps we could sit down?" *The man* proposed.

"I'm sorry…I didn't get your name." Chester muttered, glancing at his watch only to confirm what he already knew, that he would be late for work.

"I believe you knew my parents." *The man* offered.

"Perhaps, what are their names?" Chester asked impatiently.

The man approached Chester, who took a couple steps back to rest his trembling body against his car.

"I'm not sure you would recognize them by name, or even if I described them…" He paused allowing Chester time to consider his words. "Perhaps if I described the small cottage they owned on a cove in Jamestown." Now he had him, *the man* could almost hear the pounding of Chester's heart as he realized who stood before him.

"Look…" Barely able to speak above a whisper, Chester fumbled in his pocket for his car keys; "I don't know who you are or what you want, but I suggest you get in your car and leave before I call the police."

The man grinned, clearly not intimidated by Chester's threat. "Now there's an idea, why don't we call the police? I'm sure they would be very interested to know about the bodies under the porch."

"What do you want?" Chester screamed, finally finding his voice.

"Answers." *The man* said simply, moving in so close to Chester he could feel the heat of his breath.

Chester stood before his accuser, a shell of the man he once was. As he struggled to regain his composure his mind frantically searched for a way out of this mess he had gotten himself into. How was it he hadn't known the couple had a son? Why had he waited so long to confront him?

"Okay...okay." He said, motioning toward the house with a nod of his head. Taking a deep breath to steady his nerves, Chester slowly made his way back toward the front door, cautiously checking behind him to make sure *the man* didn't shoot him in the back. Not that the guy appeared to have a weapon, but just in case, he would like to see it coming. With his hand shaking violently, Chester somehow managed to unlock the door and motioned for *the man* to follow him into his study. After downing a glass of bourbon he turned to offer *the man* a glass. Shaking his head, *the man* stood firm with his arms crossed over his chest while he waited for Chester to pour himself another glass before slumping down into his chair.

Without looking up from his glass, Chester asked, "What do you want to know?"

"Why don't you just start from the beginning." *The man* suggested, leaning against the desk but remaining on guard.

Chester looked up, briefly making eye contact with *the man* before returning his gaze to his drink.

"It was the late sixties, early seventies when my research regarding lost shipwrecks brought me to the cove. I was intrigued by the mystery surrounding the wreckage and what had caused their demise. I was foolish and believed I could make a fortune if I was able to find even a fraction of their cargo. I wanted to make sure that my calculations were correct, so I hired an oceanographer and local historian to assist me in my efforts. I should have listened to their warnings...they told me not to risk everything on the mere chance that there might be something to gain, but I was too involved, too eager to heed their warnings." Chester paused, taking a long drink before continuing.

"Once they had positively confirmed my findings, I approached your parents, begging them to allow me access to the cove. I even offered them a percentage of anything I might find, but they refused. I came back again and again hoping to change their minds, even offering to buy the property outright. For nearly a year I pleaded with them to allow me access. Finally, having no other options I took out a sizable loan on my home and went to the cottage with the hope that seeing the money in cash would entice them to reconsider, but when I knocked on the door your father told me to go away. He said that if I didn't leave he would call the police. He told me to leave them alone and not to come back."

Rising from his chair, Chester stumbled over to the bar and poured himself another drink, this time moving to the window rather than face his accuser.

"It happened so fast…he had come out on the porch and grabbed me by the back of my collar. As he was attempted to escort me off the property he tripped on a tree limb that was sticking out of the sand and fell to the ground. I don't really remember exactly what happened, but I recall grabbing a large rock and bashing him in the back of the head. I don't know what came over me other than months of work and hope suddenly being ripped away. I couldn't stop, even as he lay lifeless before me, even as I heard your mother rush to his side, begging me to stop.

"When I realized what I had done, I was terrified. I couldn't go to prison…I would never survive. Not that it makes it any better, but she never saw the rock come at her as I raised it over her head. I'm not sure how long I knelt there. Somehow I managed to carry or drag them back inside. I was going to make it look like a burglary gone bad, but when I looked around I could see there was nothing there of value. Instead I pried the floorboards up from the bedroom and dug a shallow grave for their bodies. I stayed until it got dark, washing the stains from the floors and covering the bloody sand. Once I was certain any neighbors in the area were asleep for the night, I drove away.

"They had never told me they had a son and never fully explained why they weren't interested in selling the property. After a few years, the property went into foreclosure when the taxes weren't paid and my son-in-law bought it. I've been trying to get it back every since, but something or someone has always been in my way."

Relieved to have finally spoken the truth, Chester returned to his chair to wait for the consequences of his actions to be revealed.

The man listened in horror as Chester revealed the cold and brutal manner in which his parents met their death. As a POW he thought he had experienced it all and seen the worst of what mankind was capable of, but here, now, listening to his parent's killer justifying his actions as a result of disappointment and uncontrollable rage, he could barely contain himself.

It had never occurred to him that his parent's death had been an act of greed and thoughtless violence. In his mind he had simply thought that his parents had died of natural causes, and that their deaths had been concealed merely as a means to obtain the prime real estate quickly and easily. Now, however, it made sense. Of course his parents would have refused the sale of their home. He was barely eighteen when he went to Vietnam only to be captured ten days later. Despite falling gravely ill several times, he had survived and been released just prior to the withdrawal in 1973. Suffering from the mental and physical strains he had endured those many years, he had been taken to the veteran's hospital in Virginia to recover. By the time he made it back to Rhode Island, the property had been sold and his parents were nowhere to be found. Knowing how much his father loved and depended on his mother, he was certain she had died and that the loss had simply been too great for him to bear. For nearly a year he had wandered through cemeteries, hoping to find their graves. He had dug through town and hospital records hoping to find answers. It didn't take long for him to realize that something was wrong.

Chester drained the rest of the bourbon in his glass, hoping it would give him the courage he would need to face whatever this man had planned for him. His heart pounded in his chest as *the man* considered what he had said. Time stood still and the air became heavy. In his mind, Chester screamed for *the man* to say something …anything…to get on with it. And then, when every nerve in his body cried out for an end to this misery, *the man* rose, straightened his suit and walked out of the room and out the front door.

Chapter 37

Having spent the better part of the past week considering Chester's offer, Philip was now ready to announce his decision. Ultimately it had come down to the realization that though he was enjoying his adventures with Emily and thrilled at the possibility that there was more excitement to come; it was impractical to think he could survive solely on its spoils. Once he had accepted that fact, it had been an easy choice and he was actually looking forward to accepting the offer.

Dressed in his best three-piece suit of charcoal gray, Philip confidently waited outside his father-in-law's office for his secretary to arrive. Chester had left a voice mail on his phone earlier that morning announcing that he intended to take a lengthy vacation and wanted to go over a few things before he left. Philip was certain that he wouldn't be expecting him to announce his decision and he was actually looking forward to surprising the old man. Looking around him at the quiet hallway, Philip reflected on the subtle changes that had crept up on the business. In the early days, Chester would arrive well before the rest of the staff for no other reason than to hold it over their heads. He would choose his victim at random, often in front of their coworkers; and demean them for their lack of commitment to the company. He thrilled at their nervous scurrying as they attempted to bypass his office without being noticed. Now, as he checked his watch confirming it was nearly 8:00, not only was Chester not there; but neither was his secretary. To be fair, she was not immune to his belittlement games, as on more than one occasion over the years Philip recalled Chester sending her home in tears for reasons as inconsequential as his morning coffee not being hot enough. Yet, over time, perhaps out of pity for the woman who served him so dutifully; he had grown soft. Certainly it was not compassion, Philip was confident the man was incapable of that, but perhaps some sort of acknowledgement that his employees; or at least his secretary, might have some sort of a life outside of the workplace that they earned the right to enjoy.

Hearing the ring of the elevator bell, indicating the doors were about to open; Philip moved away from the wall he had been leaning on and straightened his tie. Smiling at Chester's secretary, he greeted her warmly, stepping back to allow her access to unlock the office door. Eying him curiously, she stepped into the office.

"What brings you here this early in the morning?" She asked, knowing full well he normally did everything in his power to avoid the old man.

"Actually, the old man left me a message that he wanted to go over a few things before he went on vacation." Philip responded, assisting her at removing her coat.

"Vacation? He hasn't mentioned a vacation to me."

"It sounded like a last minute decision. I'm sure he'll fill you in when he arrives." Taking a seat on the large brown leather couch in the outer office, Philip watched as she went about filling the coffee pot and preparing a tray with Chester's favorite pastries and the morning newspaper.

Picking up the latest issue of Boating Magazine, Philip flipped through the pages while Chester's secretary retrieved her voice mail and jotted down messages for her boss.

"I guess you're right." She announced.

"What's that?" Philip asked; immersed in an article that had drawn his attention.

"Mr. Eastwick is planning on a vacation. He's asked me to make arrangement for him to fly out later today."

Philip continued to read the magazine while he eavesdropped on his father-in-law's intended plans. Nearly an hour passed before Chester finally arrived, looking pale and weary. Acknowledging his presence with a nod in his direction, Chester spoke briefly with his secretary before motioning for Philip to join him in his office.

Both Philip and Chester remained silent as the secretary placed the tray of coffee and pastries between them and then quickly exited, closing the door behind her.

"Thank you for coming." Chester mumbled, reaching for his cup.

"No problem, in fact, I intended to stop by today anyhow. I've decided to accept your offer."

Philip waited for the news to sink in. Chester's reaction wasn't exactly what he expected. He had imagined Chester would be thrilled with the news, that he might pat him on the back and offer him a drink of his best bourbon, perhaps a toast to the continued success of the business. Instead, Chester merely nodded, starring blindly into his cup of coffee in deep thought.

"You do still want me to buy you out?" Philip asked, confused by Chester's solemn demeanor.

"Yes…yes, of course. I'm grateful and pleased that the business will remain in the family."

"Is everything okay, Chester? Are you ill?" He asked.

"Hmmm? No, no, everything's fine…really. I'm just tired that's all. It's been a long time since I took a vacation. I'm overdue. I'm not a young man any more."

"I understand." Philip replied. "You deserve a break. I heard your secretary mention St. Lucia."

"Yes, it's been too long since I was there. I find it quite peaceful, therapeutic really. And…now that I know the business is in good hands, I will be able to enjoy it that much more." He said, making eye contact for the first time and smiling at Philip.

As he went through a laundry list of appointments that Philip would be required to keep in his absence as well as a couple of local events that he thought might bring business their way, Philip couldn't help but notice Chester's deflated disposition. It was as though the air had literally been sucked out of him. His normally stiff back now curved, his shoulders drooping forward, not to mention his eyes that sometimes seem to peer through your very sole now looked red and tired. Philip fought the urge to ask him again if he was feeling all right, knowing that it would only anger the old man.

When Chester had taken the last sip of his coffee swallowing down the remainder of his pastry, he rose from his chair signaling the end of their meeting. In accordance, Philip too stood, shaking Chester's hand and wishing him a pleasant trip. As he neared the door to the office he turned back, intending to assure the old man that he needn't worry about anything while he was away however; seeing Chester wipe a tear that had run down his cheek and bury his face in his hands, he decided to quietly leave and closed the door behind him.

Chapter 38

A sudden change in the weather had forced Emily and Philip into hiatus and the pair had settled back into their normal work routines. Philip was consumed with the challenges of heading up the charter business and was actually succeeding in obtaining new clientele, something he was certain would please Chester greatly. As for Emily, the increased sales from book signings along with holiday shoppers had warranted the hiring of a full-time sales person, leaving her free to handle the business end of things. Though they continued to meet once a week to discuss possible sales of their finds or their intentions for future digs, they mainly talked about their personal lives and businesses.

It had been nearly a month since Chester had left town and though neither Emily nor Philip had heard from him, his name often came up in conversation. Philip remained concerned about Chester's health and state of mind, repeatedly bringing up his last encounter with the old man. Emily, of course, felt guilty at having brushed him off, wondering now if he might have given her some insight as to his reasoning for his sudden change of heart regarding the sale of his estate.

As for the estate, though the real estate agent was confident it wouldn't remain on the market for long, no offers had been made thus far. Chester's lawyer had arranged for an estate auction to sell off the vast amount of furnishings as well as a substantial collection of silver, crystal, artwork and a number of collectables. Chester had provided the attorney with a list of items that were not to be sold along with the keys to a lake house he owned in upstate New York.

According to his attorney, the location of the New York property was to remain confidential and though both Emily and Philip voiced their concerns over his odd behavior, the lawyer reassured them that Chester simply wanted to leave the hustle and bustle of Newport behind for a much smaller and quieter life at his lake house. Chester had advised him that he would remain in St. Lucia through the harsh New England winter and then intended to return to the states where he planned to live out his retirement fishing and relaxing on the lake.

"That all sounds wonderful, but why keep the location a secret? What is he hiding?" Philip argued.

"I agree with Philip." Emily interrupted, "It doesn't make any sense. It's as if he's gone into hiding. We're the closest thing to family he has, why cut us out of his life?"

"Unfortunately, only Chester himself can answer that question." His lawyer stated, "All I can do is to assure you that I personally am unaware of any reason for concern. My conversations with Chester have been upbeat and he has given me no reason to suspect anything is amiss."

"Will you at least deliver a message to Chester that we're worried about him and miss him?" Emily pleaded.

"Yes, of course."

Several weeks passed without any word from either his attorney or Chester himself and so, as life tends to do, time slipped by.

With some of the proceeds from the coin sales, Emily decided to carpet the two bedrooms in the cottage. Now that it was cold outside, she hated waking up in the morning and stepping onto the cold wood floors. On windy nights she could actually feel the cold air seep up through the cracks in the floorboards and her electric heating bill was through the roof. Weary of strangers being in her home while she was there alone, Emily scheduled the installation for a day Philip would be able to come over.

Philip arrived early to help move the furniture out of the bedrooms. The tiny spare bedroom was so sparse in furnishings they quickly moved the bed and side table out onto the porch. The bureau drawers full of clothes from Emily's room were placed in the small dining area while the bureau itself along with the remainder of the furniture joined the other things on the porch. Emily instructed Philip to sweep the floors while she filled a bucket with soap and warm water to wash them before the carpet was installed.

"Emily! Emily!" Philip screamed from the bedroom.

"What is it?" Emily yelled back as she rushed to her room to see Philip kneeling down beside an open gap in the floor.

"Call the police." Philip instructed, without taking his eyes off the hole.

"The police? What…" Emily moved closer seeing what Philip saw for the first time. "Oh my God." She whispered, clasping her hands over her mouth.

"Go!" Philip shouted, pushing his hand against her calf to get her moving.

While Emily called the police, Philip began to pry more of the floorboards off, opening the gap wider. He had been sweeping the floor when the bristles had gotten caught on the edge of one board that was slightly raised from the others. When he pulled on the handle to dislodge the broom, the board had lifted revealing the horror below. By the time Emily returned to the room Philip had removed a large section of flooring, exposing the remains of not one but two skeletons.

"Oh my God, Philip…who are they?" Emily whispered in a shaky voice.

"I don't know," Philip said, "but whoever they are, someone went to a great deal of trouble to make sure they wouldn't be found."

In what seemed like no time at all, the cottage was swarming with members of both the local Jamestown Police as well as the state police's BCI unit. As Philip and Emily sat by watching and waiting in silence, the officers photographed the ever-widening hole. While detectives used crowbars to pry more of the floorboards away, exposing a larger area, others laid out a tarp to collect evidence on. Emily sunk into the couch, wringing her hands nervously while Philip was interviewed in the tiny kitchen. Her own interview had lasted only ten minutes as she had little to offer in the way of information as to whom the individuals buried under her bedroom floor might be.

Philip, it seemed, would be far more helpful in detailing the history of the property and so had been questioned for nearly an hour before returning to the living room and joining her on the couch. At some point, the carpet installers had arrived and been turned away by an officer standing guard outside the property. The remains of the two individuals were removed from the cottage in body bags along with several smaller bags containing evidence.

After nearly five hours of activity all that remained was one uniformed officer who was taping off the room along with the lead detective who approached Philip and Emily.

"It looks like we have everything we need here. I'm going to ask that you stay out of the room until we've determined we've gathered all the evidence.

Once I give the all clear you can go ahead and replace the floorboards and install the carpeting as you planned."

Emily merely nodded her head, still in shock over the day's events.

"You'll contact me when you've located the paperwork from your original purchase?" The detective asked.

"Yes…yes I'll bring it by tomorrow." Philip confirmed.

"Very well then, I suggest you spend the night at a friends or a hotel. Situations like this can be quite upsetting. It's unlikely you'll get much sleep tonight." The detective said, addressing Emily.

Again, Emily merely nodded her understanding.

"I'll see to her comfort." Philip assured the detective, showing him to the door where the uniformed officer was waiting. "Thank you for everything."

Philip watched as the two officers returned to their vehicles and drove away before returning to Emily's side. The events of the day had finally taken their toll and Emily began to weep openly. Wrapping his arms around her, Philip rocked back and forth while stroking her hair and whispering reassurances. For him, this was unfamiliar territory and he wasn't sure what to say if anything so he simply held her and mumbled that everything would be okay and to go ahead and let it all out. Slowly Emily's cries turned to tiny hiccups and soft sighs and Philip left her side to make her a cup of tea and retrieve a box of tissues from the bathroom.

Philip sat in silence as Emily drank her tea and settled her nerves before suggesting that she pack an overnight bag and spend the night at his place. Emily quickly accepted his offer, grabbing a small suitcase from the hall closet and stuffing a few articles of clothing from her bureau drawers as well as some toiletries inside. The very thought of having lived in a house with two bodies buried beneath it sent chills up her spine, not to mention the fact that they were most certainly murdered.

As for Philip, he continued to assure Emily that they would get to the bottom of it and that whatever happened there had occurred long ago and certainly she had no reason to be afraid. Grateful for his common sense attitude and emotional support, Emily relaxed and was even able to eventually fall asleep after a light meal and a hot bath.

Chapter 39

Nearly a month had passed since the discovery of the two bodies buried beneath the cottage and the police were no closer to resolving the crime. The paperwork Philip had provided had been a dead end seeing that the property had been turned over to the town and did not name the previous owners. Furthermore, the bank, a once celebrated Rhode Island icon, was now defunct and obtaining its records required involvement from the federal government. Though the Attorney General's office assured the police that they would eventually get their answers, it required a lengthy process of subpoenas and court battles. Their only hope would be if someone in the public could provide the information.

Naturally it would have been much simpler if the town records were available, however a hurricane in the '80's had flooded the basement of the building that housed those documents destroying everything. Though most towns had begun storing their documents on hard drives, small towns like Jamestown were reluctant to make the change. The backlash from the taxpayers once hearing the news that the records had been destroyed had forced their hands and they were now an example to other communities throughout the state of what happens when you don't keep up with technology.

It was a long shot considering that no one had come forward when the newspapers had reported the grisly discovery however the local police had decided it was worth the effort to post a public notice requesting information pertaining to the identity of the previous owners of the property. It was their hope that they might be able to interview the owners to see if they had any knowledge of the deceased or who might have built the structure itself. Though the medical examiner had determined the cause of death to be homicide, it was still possible that someone might remember something about the previous owners that might lead to their identity. The fact that the property had fallen into the hands of the town suggested that the owners had simply abandoned the property, perhaps through no fault of their own.

Ultimately, their efforts paid off when several weeks into the investigation a stranger walked into the Jamestown Police Station and asked to speak with the detective in charge of the investigation. Identifying himself as Theodore Manchester of Newport Rhode Island, the man proceeded to provide the detective with the information they had been looking for.

According to the man, his parents, Harriet and Winston Manchester, were the original owners and occupants of the cottage. Originally purchased as a summer home for the wealthy couple, they had made it their permanent residence when his father had retired. Describing his parents as intelligent but simple people, he explained that they were looking forward to a quiet life when he left home to fight in Vietnam. Having married late in life and having him; an only child, in their mid 40s, they had settled into retirement shortly after he graduated from high school. Theo, as his friends called him; explained how he had been captured by enemy troops and been held as a prisoner of war before being released and returned to the United States where he spent time at a VA hospital. By the time he returned to Rhode Island, he explained, his parents were no longer the owners of the property and he had never been able to locate them.

As the detective listened to the man's tale, he couldn't help but feel he was leaving something out. Why hadn't he reported them missing? Wasn't a neighbor or a friend checking in on them? Theo acknowledged that he probably should have contacted the police but had decided instead to hire a private investigator that was unable to come up with any leads. Most of their friends, he explained had retired to other parts of the country or were deceased by the time he returned from the war and those that were around had simply lost touch with his parents. Though the home had been sold to pay off the taxes owed to the town, the courts eventually declared the missing couple deceased and he had inherited their sizable bank accounts.

After agreeing to provide a DNA sample to compare with the remains and presenting the detective with information pertaining to his employment, address and phone numbers Theo asked if he might contact the current owners of the property to inquire as to whether or not they still had anything belonging to his parents. The detective advised Theo that he would contact the owner and provide her with his information, but it was up to her whether or not she would be willing to meet with him.

Despite his initial doubts, the information seemed to check out regarding Theodore Manchester's service in the military as well as his after care at the VA hospital, therefore eliminating him as a suspect in the crime. Although he still awaited the results of the DNA tests, the detective was confident that the remains would be those of the man's parents. Now he just needed to figure out who killed them and why. As promised he delivered the gentleman's information to Emily, informing her of the information the man had provided and advising her to be cautious and meet him in public rather than at the cottage.

Though Emily was eager to meet the man who might be able to shed some light into the couple's mysterious deaths, Philip was cautiously pessimistic about the whole thing. What if he wanted to reestablish ownership of the property? What if he was dangerous? What if he was a con man who had simply heard of their recent good fortune and wanted to take advantage of the situation?

But Emily persisted, undeterred and hopeful that she might be able to put closure on the matter. Eventually Philip gave in, accepting the fact that Emily's mind was not to be changed; and contacted the man.

Emily and Philip arrived at the restaurant early, requesting a quiet table in the back and advising the hostess that they were expected a third party to join them. Emily felt a tingle of excitement in anticipation of meeting the gentleman and her arms were covered in goose bumps. As she sipped her wine nervously, Philip pulled at the knot in his tie and twitched his leg until Emily placed her hand on his thigh to stop him from bouncing right out of his seat. Realizing what he had been doing, he apologized and suggested they select an appetizer from the menu to distract them from the impending meeting. They had just placed the order when the hostess approached the table with a gentleman close at her heals. Philip rose from his chair to greet the man.

"You must be Theodore...my name is Philip... Philip Bohman and this lovely young lady is Emily Gaudet, the current owner of the property."

Theo shook Philip's hand and nodded a hello to Emily, "Please...call me Theo."

"Theo it is." Emily agreed, "Please sit down, would you care for a drink?"

The waiter approached the table, noting the addition of a third party and took his drink order before quickly departing to attend to another table.

A brief yet awkward silence fell over the table while they each searched for an easy way to begin the uncomfortable conversation. Ultimately it was Theo who addressed the subject.

"I want to thank you both for agreeing to meet with me. I've considered simply knocking on your door many times over the years and introducing myself. The truth is…I've suspected for some time that my parents met with foul play, however it wasn't until recently that my fears were confirmed."

Emily reached across the table placing her hand on top of the strangers.

"I'm so sorry for your loss." She said, squeezing his hand before returning it to her lap.

"Thank you. I realize what I'm about to tell you might be shocking, but I'm going to take a leap of faith and hope that you'll hear me out." Again he paused to collect his thoughts while both Philip and Emily looked at each other in confusion.

"When I returned to Rhode Island after the war I went to the cottage to look for my parents. I had been a prisoner of war for several years and then spent time recuperating at a VA hospital before returning home. When I arrived I found a young woman was living there by the name of Sarah Eastwick. I asked her what had become of my parents but it was obvious she didn't know anything. She told me that her sister had given her the property as a gift and advised me that her sister had passed away. I thought perhaps my parents had simply died during my long absence and so I began to dig through newspaper archives looking for any mention of their deaths.

"When my efforts failed, I went to the town hall to inquire about the sale of the property and was informed that the town had taken possession of the property for back taxes and their bank had sold the property to Katherine Bohman who had later transferred ownership to Sarah Eastwick. It didn't make any sense. My parents had plenty of money and even if they passed away, their lawyers would have seen that the property was held in trust. At that point I knew something was wrong.

"I was familiar with the Eastwick name and the power they held within the town and was afraid if I went to the authorities I too might be in danger. Whatever the reason for my parents disappearance, I felt it had something to do with the property. After all, it was prime real estate even by those days' standards.

"I decided to hire an investigator; a nobody that wouldn't draw attention and had no obvious connections to the property or the Eastwick family. For years he kept an eye on the property, reporting back to me with anything he thought seemed out of the ordinary while I continued to look for leads. I spent years combing through the local cemeteries looking for my parent's plots, but of course never found them.

"I had all but given up hope when I saw the obituary of Sarah Eastwick. I thought that if I could buy the property, perhaps I would be able to dig around. I was certain that if they were murdered, their bodies were somewhere on the property. I continued to watch for an announcement that the property was back on the market and was prepared to pay whatever was asked to get it back.

"It was around that time that my informant advised me that an old man was poking around the area and appeared to be looking for something. He watched while the old man dug around the beach, on the side of the property and close to the shore. At first he thought he was digging a grave but then as he continued to monitor his activity it appeared as though he was searching for something. When the cold weather set in he would disappear not to return until the following spring. Then a young man came upon the scene and he seemed to be cleaning up the property and preparing to move in.

"At first I was furious. I had been diligent about checking the real estate ads for new listings. How could I have missed it? I went back to the town hall to find out who the new owner was and found out it was a man named Chase Bohman. According to the records, the property had been transferred to him upon the death of Sarah Eastwick.

"I wondered what it was about the property that continued to intrigue the old man and why my informant continued to advise me that he lurked around the property searching for something. He seemed to somehow be privy to the other man's schedule and knew that he was only there on the weekends and so they were never present at the same time. That is…not until that weekend."

Both Emily and Philip had sat quietly listening to Theo recite the history of the property, filling in blanks and at times providing them with information at least Philip was already aware of. Now, however, they both noticeably stiffened, preparing themselves for what he was about to say.

"On that particular day, my informant had phoned me to announce that he had observed the old man peering through the back windows of the cottage while the younger man was inside. Fearful for his safety, I advised my guy to sit tight and keep an eye on things from a distance. I told him that if he thought the young man was in immediate danger he was to place an anonymous call to 911 and get out of there. I remember pacing back and forth in my apartment waiting to hear back from him as the day turned into night. Finally he called me and said that the young man had left in his car and that it appeared the old man had followed. I, of course assumed everything was alright and settled down for the night.

"It wasn't until the next day when I heard Chase Bohman had gone off the road, that I knew in my heart of hearts that the old man was somehow responsible."

"That's impossible." Emily cried, "Chester never would have hurt Chase, he loved him." She looked to Philip for backup but he simply lowered his head.

"Philip? Philip…you don't really believe Chester would have done something to hurt Chase?"

Philip looked into her eyes, seeing the raw pain that he too was feeling. "He's not the man you think he is, Emily."

"No…no, I refuse to believe it." Emily cried, pushing back her chair and running from the table.

Philip also rose, tossing a few bills on the table to cover the tab. "I have to go after her, I'll call you."

Theo watched as Philip rushed to catch up with Emily who had already exited the restaurant. Perhaps he shouldn't have revealed so much so fast, but then again…the nightmare had gone on far too long already. It was time Chester pay for his sins.

Chapter 40

Several days passed as Emily struggled to come to grips with the possibility that Chester may have been responsible for Chase's accident and ultimately his death. Though Philip had followed her out of the restaurant and pleaded with her to hear Theo out, she had refused, telling him she needed to be alone. In the days that followed, Philip continued to call her, even stopping by the shop, but her associate had informed him that Emily was taking a few days off and didn't want to be disturbed. Although he respected her wishes, Philip worried that if he allowed her to wallow in grief for too long, it would be a setback to the progress she had made with putting the past behind her. And so, on the seventh day of her solitude, he came knocking at her door, refusing to leave until she allowed him inside to speak with her.

"Fine, you can come in," Emily agreed, "but I'm not ready to believe that Chester would intentionally harm his grandson."

"I understand why you might be reluctant to believe a total stranger, but I know Chester well enough to concede that he is capable of just about anything he sets his mind to."

Emily had moved to the kitchen where she was filling the teapot with water, which was now over-flowing back into the sink. Philip reached past her to take the pot from her and shut off the faucet.

"Listen," He said, taking her by the hands and directing her back to the living room where he motioned for her to sit. "I spent nearly my entire life trying to please Chester, putting up with his insults and innuendos, all the while biting my tongue while I watched everyone around him cower at his often violent temper. I watched as his wife drank herself to death, as the women in the office ran out in tears and as he dismissed those who were no longer of any use to him with no thought at all to how it would affect their families. So believe me when I tell you…it's not so much of a stretch to think that he might be capable of harming his own grandson if he got in the way of something he wanted or became aware of something that might send him to prison.

"What Theo said makes sense. Chester wanted that property; that I know for a fact. If the Manchester's were unwilling to part with it, I wouldn't put it past him to eliminate them. He had no way of knowing Katherine was going to buy it before he had a chance. Then once she signed the property over to Sarah, he had no choice but to sit tight. Sarah never cared about material things, she was never a threat to him, and in fact she unknowingly was doing the work for him by playing the treasure hunter. After she died, he was easily able to resume his work until Chase decided to make use of the property. It stands to reason that he would become concerned that his secrets would be revealed. Even if Chase never discovered the bodies, the very fact that he would no longer have access to the property would be enough to send him over the edge."

"But why?" Emily cried, choking back tears. "Why not just ask Chase – they had a good relationship? It just doesn't make sense."

"I don't know, but I have to wonder if all this has something to do with his decision to sell the company and go into hiding. It's the only thing that makes sense. I think we need to finish hearing Theo out. Obviously the man knows a great deal more than we do about Chester."

Emily reluctantly agreed and Philip phoned the man and arranged for him to meet them the following evening at his office in Newport. Emily spent the day mentally preparing herself for whatever she was about to learn. The weather had taken a turn for the worse and a combination of driving sleet and rain had blanketed the area. The local news was reporting several power outages and accidents throughout the area and recommended that people stay off the roads if at all possible.

Though she was anxious to get the meeting over with, she realized whatever she might learn wouldn't be worth risking her life for so she picked up the phone and called Philip, suggesting they reschedule for the following evening.

"That's a good idea, I haven't heard the weather report but the traffic outside my window is at a virtual standstill. I'll call Theo and make the arrangements."

Relieved that she was able to at least postpone a meeting she was not looking forward to, Emily changed into a pair of comfortable stretch pants and a baggy t-shirt that had once belonged to Chase. A warm grilled cheese sandwich and a hot bowl of tomato soup was just what she needed to take the edge off and so she went about preparing her dinner, more relaxed than she had felt in days.

She had just placed her tray of food on a small portable table she often used to eat on in the living room when she heard something or someone tapping at the front door. Due to the harsh conditions outside, Emily assured herself that it was simply a loose shingle or the cover from the metal mailbox that was bolted to the side of the door and she ignored it and sat down to eat. Flipping through the channels, she settled on the evening news and began to eat when her front door suddenly burst open with an enormous gust of wind and slammed against the closet door nearby. Practically jumping out of her seat and nearly toppling over her tray of food, she rushed to the door to close it just in time to see a car pull out of her driveway. Nervously grasping the door she pushed it forcefully to lock it in place, however a small package prevented it from closing. Reaching down to retrieve the package she again pressed against the door, this time successfully securing it.

Leaning against the now closed door she stopped to catch her breath and looked down at the manila envelope that simply read "Emily" in handwriting. Still shaking from the unnerving interruption, Emily moved to the couch, no longer interested in the soup and sandwich she had planned to eat only moments ago.

With her hands shaking she turned the envelope over and pinched the metal tabs to unfasten it and retrieve its contents. Inside she found a handwritten note along with a journal. The note simply read:

All the answers you seek will be found in these pages

Emily ran her hand over the words as if that might reveal some hidden message or the identity of its author. Flipping open the cover of the journal she found the delicate handwriting of a woman with an inscription:

This Diary Belongs to Sarah

Without reading them, she flipped through the pages filled with delicate handwriting and whimsical drawings of mermaids, seashells and various depictions of sea life. Suddenly Emily recalled Chester mentioning a journal he had given Sarah to catalog her treasure-hunting hobby and she wondered if perhaps this was it. Now that she thought about it, she didn't recall seeing it in the box of items she had originally given to Chester of Sarah's belongings or amongst the items that she had held onto.

Picking up the phone she dialed Philip's number, hoping she would be able to reach him before he left his office for the evening.

"Hello?" He answered.

"Philip it's me... Emily."

"Emily? Is everything okay?" He asked nervously.

"Yes...um, I'm not sure. I know the weather's bad, but is there any way you can come out here?" She pleaded.

"Of course, I was just heading out. I can be there in half an hour." He promised.

When he arrived, Emily had been watching from the window and opened the door before he had a chance to knock.

"What is it?" He asked, looking around her in a panic to see if anyone else was there.

Describing what happened, Emily explained that she wasn't certain if the person who dropped off the package was Chester or someone else and that the weather was too bad for her to get a good look at the car before it drove away.

"Well I guess there's only one way to find out." Philip said, holding up the journal.

For nearly two hours Philip flipped through the pages as Emily read over his shoulder, sometimes stopping him from turning the page so that she could catch up. As he turned the final page to find an eerie sketch of the cottage they both felt a tingle of nerves crawl up their spines.

"Are you okay?" Emily asked softly, seeing the pain in Philip's eyes.

Philip placed the book on the coffee table and moved to the window, wrapping his hands behind his back and starring hard into the night. Emily waited patiently for him to respond.

"I don't know how to feel." He whispered, turning to face her. "I had no idea she loved me so much or that she wanted the three of us to be a family. If I had known … things could have been so much different for us, for Chase. I thought I was doing the right thing in staying away, that I was giving Chase the mother he so desperately needed and deserved."

"Why do you think she never told you?" Emily asked.

"Probably the same reason I stayed away…Chester. He had this vision of what life was supposed to be and God help anyone that challenged that vision. Katherine was just like him, selfish and obstinate with an over inflated sense of entitlement. It wasn't just about having what they wanted; it was about taking what others had just to see them suffer. The mere notion that I might have feelings for Sarah and Katherine took my dream away from me, but it wasn't enough to take it, she had to give it to someone close to me so that it would always be just out of reach but forever in sight."

"But what was in it for Chester? If it was him that dropped off this journal, what does he mean we will find all our answers in its pages?" Emily asked picking up the journal and flipping through the pages for something she was certain they had missed.

"I'm certain it was Chester who dropped it off. I recognize the handwriting. I think it's his way of explaining why he did what he did. He obviously feels he was saving her from her sister's fate. I've told you before he suspects me as having something to do with her death. The truth is…he's right."

Philip waited for Emily to respond, to bolt in fear or scream in horror, but she simply looked in his eyes with compassion. Her empathy gave him the confidence to go on and he spoke for the first time in his life the truth about what happened on that night. When he was done, Emily rose from her position on the couch and approached him, looking into his eyes for a moment then wrapping her arms around him in an embrace.

"Oh Philip, it wasn't your fault. She was baiting you, she wanted you to challenge her, she wanted to push you and see how far she could go. I can't imagine what it was like being married to a woman like that, to constantly be put down. As far as I'm concerned, she got what she deserved. It's not like you pushed her to her death, she lost her footing, and if she hadn't been following you in the first place, it never would have happened."

"That's kind of you to say and it's something I've tried to convince myself of for years, but the truth is I could have simply walked away. I knew exactly what would happen when I stepped forward and I did it anyway."

"That may be true Philip, but I still think she had it coming to her and I think you did Chase a tremendous favor. Growing up with Sarah as his mother figure gave him the stimulation he needed to become the successful writer that he became. Who knows what would have become of him if Katherine had raised him."

"I guess you're right...I want to believe that." Philip muttered sinking back onto the couch.

"So why do you suppose Chester would want me to read this? I still don't see how it answers anything." Emily pondered, picking up the journal once again.

"I think in his own sick way, Chester is trying to turn you against me. I think he knew Theo was about to play his hand and that you would find out about his possible involvement in Chase's death and he thought he might trick you into believing it was me and not him that you should be afraid of. I think that he has come to realize that it's too late to repair the damage he has done to our relationship and you are his only hope for family in these last years of his life."

Emily considered Philips words. It was difficult to understand how anyone could be so cruel as to do the things Chester had done to his family. He had destroyed so many lives for his selfish desires. And for what? This man had become like a grandfather to her, someone she could share memories of Chase with, who she could turn to for support. How could the man that she had grown to love be such a monster?

"What should we do?" Emily asked, accepting the truth.

"I think we need to meet with Theo, to find out what else he knows. If he is responsible for Chase's death, he needs to pay."

Agreeing with Philip, Emily insisted he stay the night, offering him the spare bedroom so he wouldn't have to travel in the storm. He agreed, stating there was no way he would have allowed her to spend the night alone anyway.

Chapter 41

The following morning Emily awoke confident for the first time in days that there might finally be an end in sight to the horrible nightmare she had been living these past few months. By the time she showered and dressed she found Philip outside chipping away at the ice that was caked on his car. Grabbing her parka from the hallway closet, along with a sturdy pair of boots, she stopped at her car to retrieve her ice scrapper before approaching his vehicle.

"Good morning." She called out over the roar of his engine and the local news being broadcast from his radio. "Need a little help?" She asked, holding up her ice scrapper.

"Good morning and yes, I will gladly accept your assistance. There has to be at least a half inch of ice on here." Philip responded, stopping what he was doing to give her a quick hug.

As they scrapped the windows, Philip reconfirmed their plan to meet with Theo later that evening at his office. Assuring him that she would be there, Emily explained that she intended to go to the shop to get some work done as well as avoid being alone in the cottage in case there was another unannounced visit from Chester. After scrapping all of Philip's car windows they moved on to Emily's car, which seemed to have somehow been spared from the full force of the driving rain and sleet. Though the windows still required scrapping, the layer of ice was much thinner and they completed the task in no time.

Thanking her for her assistance and advising her to call his cell phone if she even suspected there was something amiss, Emily watched as Philip drove away.

After a quick breakfast of toast and coffee, Emily grabbed her bag and was on her way to Newport. Having taken more time off than she had intended, she knew there would be mounds of paperwork to catch up on when she got there. She was pleased to see that there were already several customers browsing the shelves when she arrived at a little past ten o'clock. Her floor manager joined her in her office to go over the sales numbers, which were good considering the off-season. All in all, Emily was very pleased with the business she had made for herself and was confident that if she continued to be diligent the shop would be around for many years to come.

After the meeting with her floor manager and walking through the shop to admire the new displays, Emily returned to her office to go through her mail. Sorting the invoices from the marketing material forwarded to her by the various distributors she dealt with, Emily made quick work of separating the junk from the things she needed to further consider. Having instructed her assistant to interrupt her when she was ready to go to lunch, she was surprised by how quickly the time seemed to have gone by when she saw her standing at her door.

"Is it lunchtime already?" Emily asked.

"I'm afraid so, can I bring you back anything?" The girl asked, always eager to please her boss.

"If you wouldn't mind, I'd love a salad."

After retrieving money from her bag and sending her assistant on her way, Emily moved to the front of the store to cover the floor. Several groups of customers stopped by on their lunch breaks to inquire about upcoming events and purchase books. More than one customer complimented her on her choice of material, stating that they too were fond of the classics. Emily had recently purchased new editions of her favorite classics and bundled them together as a way to encourage a new generation of readers to be swept away by the author's stories. Each bundle catered to a different genre and seemed to be flying off the shelves. Especially popular were the bundle of classics by Edgar Allan Poe. The younger readers seemed to be obsessed these days with the macabre.

When her assistant returned with her lunch, Emily retreated back to her office to continue her work paying invoices and weeding through the stack of mail. By three o'clock she had caught up on the most pressing issues and joined her assistant up front.

"Why don't you call it an early day, I'll cover you for the rest of the day." She informed the assistant.

"Are you sure?" The girl asked, excited at the prospect of leaving early enough to enjoy a few hours of sunlight before the winter night set in.

"I'm sure, now go." Emily insisted, playfully pushing the girl toward the door. "And don't waste it, go shopping or something." Watching the girl as she quickly crossed the street in the direction of a new clothing establishment, Emily smiled at the spring in the girl's step. How many years had it been since she was that young? She remembered those summers working on the strip, watching the tourists go in and out of shops, their arms full of bags, joyfully chatting with their companions. She recalled how excited she would be when she got an unexpected afternoon off to enjoy the things they did, if only for a short time. It was like that last day of school when the final bell rings and you know the possibilities are endless for the summer. Somehow, one loses that sense of wonder, as they grow older.

The remainder of the afternoon was fairly quiet and Emily was considering closing the shop early when the little bell attached to the door jingled, signaling she had a customer. She had been sitting in Chase's Corner watching the sidewalk traffic as the sun began to go down and so she rose to greet her customer, grateful for the interruption.

"Welcome to…" She began and then seeing Chester standing before her, stopped in her tracks.

Before her stood the man she had, not so long ago; thought of as a grandfather, but now terrified her. Without saying a word, he turned and locked the door, flipping the cardboard sign to signify the shop was closed. Emily stood motionless, her eyes darting around her for a way to escape. Regrettably her cell phone was sitting on her desk at the back of the shop.

"I think we need to talk." Chester stated, moving toward her. "Why don't we go back to your office?" It wasn't really a suggestion, as he grabbed her elbow and directed her toward the back.

Emily was certain she could get away from him if she needed to; all she needed to do was to get up the nerve or distract him long enough to make a run for the side door. Instead though, she allowed him to escort her into her office and deposit her behind her desk before he went around and sat on the other side. Though he had clearly lost a few pounds since she last saw him, his tanned face gave him a healthy appearance making him seem somewhat younger and perhaps stronger.

Emily cleared her throat preparing herself to speak. "What do you want, Chester?"

"Clearly, Philip has turned you against me." He stated, avoiding her question. "I thought perhaps that might happen when I left town. Did you read Sarah's journal?"

"Yes, we did, though I'm not sure what you expected me to learn from it. I was already aware of Philip's feelings toward Sarah. I find it sad, really."

"Sad…sad for whom?" Chester lashed out.

"Sad for both of them. Sad that they were never able to act on their feelings, sad that they both were forced to push those feelings aside and live a lonely existence when they could have been happy. Sad that Chase never knew the joy of having parents who loved each other and loved him."

Emily rose, wiping a tear that had escaped and was running down her cheek.

"Philip didn't deserve to be happy. I wasn't going to allow him to destroy and possibly kill another child of mine. He killed Katherine, of that I'm certain."

"What about you? What about that couple you killed? What about the wife you claimed to have loved but shoved aside? What about Chase?"

Emily looked into Chester's cold eyes and saw for the first time the man that Philip had been trying to describe all this time. A man so evil he would stop at nothing to get what he wanted, so wicked he destroyed everything and everyone in his path.

Chester quickly rose from his chair, covering the distance between himself and Emily so fast that she barely had time to react and only then she merely stepped back, pressing her back against the wall. Emily frantically looked around her for something she might use as a weapon when Chester grabbed her by the arms, shoving her hard against the wall before grabbing the back of her head and slamming her face into the upright file cabinet beside her. As she lost consciousness, her eyes fell on the picture of her and Chase and she prayed that if she died, he would be there waiting for her.

Chapter 42

It was nearly 6:30 and Philip nervously rang Emily's phone for the third time. It wasn't like her to be late and considering what happened the night before, he was more than a little concerned for her wellbeing.

Theo had arrived promptly at 6:00 o'clock, having only to take the elevator up to Philip's office from his own in the same building. How odd it was that they had all worked so close to each other all these years, seeing each other on a daily basis and never realizing their connection. It was true what they said about it being a small world; they were the perfect example.

Philip had offered Theo a glass of bourbon, which he gratefully accepted to take the edge off and they had exchanged small talk while waiting for Emily to arrive. When it became apparent that she was running late and when they had run out of pleasantries to exchange, Philip had proceeded to call her. Her phone rang several times before going to voice mail, indicating her phone was on but she was unable to answer it. Thinking perhaps she was tied up with last minute customers, Philip gave her another five minutes before trying her office phone. Again the phone rang several times before the answering machine clicked on and he left a message.

Now, a half hour past the time they were scheduled to meet, Philip attempted again to reach her on her cell phone, but again it went to voice mail. Turning to Theo who also seemed concerned now he stated what they both were thinking.

"Something's wrong."

"You don't suppose she went home and forgot about our meeting?" Theo suggesting, realizing as he said it how unlikely it was.

"I doubt it," Philip said, shaking his head, "especially after what happened last night."

Describing the events of the previous night, Philip wrung his hands. By the time he had Theo up to date it was nearly 6:45 and they both agreed they needed to go look for her. Theo insisted on driving as Philip was clearly too upset to focus and they quickly made their way to the shop. Parking his car on a side street, they walked the short distance to the shop. First checking the front door and seeing that the "Closed" sign was in place and the door was locked, they moved to the side entrance, noting her car was still parked in the alley.

Philip pounded loudly on the locked door calling out for Emily, but there was no response.

"I think we should call the police." Theo said, "Something is definitely not right about this."

Agreeing, Philip called 911 and they waited for an officer to meet them, directing him to the small alley. After quickly explaining their fears that she may be in danger and waiting while the officer also attempted to call her out, they stood back as he kicked in the door and instructed them to wait outside while he searched the place. A tense few minutes passed while Philip and Theo nervously waited for the officer to return to the alley. After calling for BCI and an additional unit to join him, he addressed the two men.

"It looks like there was a struggle back in the office. I've called for our BCI unit to come out and do their thing and a detective is on his way. He'll want to get as much information from you two as you can provide. In the meantime I'm going to ask you to take a seat in the back of my cruiser so that you don't disturb any possible evidence."

"Can you call the Jamestown Police Department and have someone go over to her place and check it out?" Philip pleaded.

"Of course, what's the address?" The officer asked as he escorted them back to his vehicle.

A half hour later, after being transported to the police station, Philip and Theo provided the detective with as much information as they deemed necessary to track down Chester. Though neither of them was willing to divulge the entire story, they informed the detective of the events surrounding the discovery of the bodies and their belief that Chester was behind their deaths. A call was placed to Chester's attorney who provided the detective with information pertaining to Chester's last known whereabouts as well as the address to his lake house.

Several calls were placed to the various police departments to be on the lookout for Chester and to consider him dangerous. A description and photo of Emily was provided as well. As the hours passed without word, Philip anxiously paced the floor of the interrogation room while Theo attempted to calm his nerves with encouraging words.

"He's an old man...she's young and in good shape. Even if he was somehow able to take her down, I suspect she wouldn't be down for long. She's a smart girl, she'll get through this." Somehow though, he wasn't sure he was convincing even himself. He knew what Chester was capable of and that there was no limit to the lengths he would go to in order to protect his interests.

As they continued to wait, the detective kept them apprised of the efforts being made. Though she had not been located, the fact that she had been removed from the location of the struggle meant she was most likely still alive. By daybreak he had informed the men that both the Jamestown cottage as well as the lake house has turned up empty and that it didn't appear as though anything was disturbed at either location. A search of the vessels owned by Excursion Charters was currently underway and the Coast Guard had been placed on alert to prevent any of the boats from leaving dock.

At some point in the morning, the detective's clerk had come in with a tray of donuts and a decanter of coffee and though Philip insisted he wasn't hungry, Theo encouraged him to eat something to keep up his strength.

As the investigation continued, Philip provided whatever information he could to assist in the search, hoping that even the smallest of details would sway the investigation in the right direction. The detective assured the men that no detail was too small and that every bit of information they could provide would be useful.

By nightfall, they were no closer to finding Chester or Emily and the detective insisted the men go home and get some sleep, promising he would call them if he had any news before the morning. Though Philip doubted he was likely to get any sleep, he agreed to go home and an officer was instructed to return Theo to his vehicle left behind near the shop and Philip to his own in the basement garage of his office building.

Chapter 43

Emily struggled to open her eyes. A blinding headache as well as the swelling from her broken nose, made it nearly impossible for her to tolerate even the dim light that she knew surrounded her. A soft whimper escaped her lips as she attempted to sit up and was shoved back to the floor by a hard object to the shoulder. Crying out in pain, she laid back down on what seemed to be a cement floor.

At some point during the night she remembered waking up and thinking she had been buried alive. As she fought back the panic she felt the motion of a vehicle and realized she was in the trunk of a car...Chester's car. She vaguely recalled the confrontation at her shop and him shoving her against the wall before smashing her face into the file cabinet. After that, she had apparently blacked out. How long had she been out? Where was he taking her? She had to try to stay calm if she wanted to survive.

The next time she woke up she was being carried down a flight a stairs. The light burned through her lids and her head throbbed as the elderly man struggled to deposit her on the cold hard floor. She had pretended to be passed out as she listened to him attempt to calm his breathing. Maybe he would have a heart attack and she could escape.

Evidently she had passed out again before she was able to react and now she had no idea how long she had been held captive or where she might be. She licked her dry lips and swallowed before attempting to speak.

"Chester? Is that you?" She asked.

"Who else would it be?" He answered sarcastically. "It would be best if you remain calm. I'll get you some water."

Nodding her head, Emily slowly opened her eyes, which immediately began to water, blurring her vision. Each time she squinted, attempting to clear her eyes, the skin surrounding her swollen nose tightened causing her to cry out in pain. Her face was so swollen she could see her bulging cheeks below her eyes. Her hands and feet had been bound with duct tape preventing her from moving freely.

Chester returned to the room and placed a glass of water to her lips instructing her to drink it slowly so she didn't choke. After she had drunk about half a glass, he pulled it away from her lips. Pulling a chair up in front of her, he lifted her to the seat before sitting down himself.

"So...what should we do now?" He asked, tapping the handle of a shotgun on the floor.

"Chester please...if you ever had any feelings for me at all...and I think you did, please let me go." Emily begged.

"Now why would I do that...clearly you've decided I'm guilty of a number of crimes. Why on earth would I let you go?"

Emily struggled to think of anything that might sway Chester's mind.

"At least explain to me why...if I can't convince you to let me go, at least tell me what really happened to Chase. I need to know...please."

Though Chester looked directly at her, it was as though he looked through her as he considered her request.

"Very well, I guess I owe you that." Rising from his chair, Chester moved toward the wall, leaning his back against it for support while still holding onto the shotgun.

"I guess you know most of the story…at least someone's version of events. I had finally resumed my search of the property when Chase showed up to claim ownership. I arrived one Sunday to find him there. He told me that he intended to clean up the cottage so that you and he could use it as a summer retreat. I had heard mumblings that your relationship had gotten serious and that he had proposed to you and I knew it was only a matter of time before I would once again lose access to the property.

"I made him a ridiculous offer to buy the property from him but he declined the offer telling me that his memories of the cottage and the time he spent there were priceless and that he wouldn't consider selling it. As I had with the previous owners I continued to press him to change his mind but it only resulted in pushing him further away.

"I had hoped that he would change his mind, that perhaps we could come to some amicable solution whereby we shared the property and so I revealed my reason for wanting the land. He laughed at me…told me I was a foolish old man, told me that there was no treasure, that he had witnessed Sarah hiding the supposed treasure herself and that I had wasted my life on a pipe dream.

"I was furious and embarrassed by his suggestion that my research had been somehow flawed. All the years that I had sacrificed, all the money I had spent in an effort to reach my goal. I refused to consider it was merely the fantasy of a foolish man. So I went there the following Sunday and I watched him from outside, desperate to think of some way to convince him he was wrong…that there was treasure to be found. I watched through the bedroom window as he pulled a box out of the closet and found the coins and I saw the look on his face when he realized what I had been saying was true.

"As he carefully inspected each coin, I saw the excitement grow within him and I panicked. I thought that he was going to screw me and I couldn't allow it. I followed him down the long drive way. I was beeping my horn, trying to signal him to stop so that we could talk. Maybe he thought I was going to run him off the road, maybe he didn't realize it was me...I don't know. All I know is he drove faster, so I drove faster and by the time I got to the main road he was gone. It wasn't until you called me that I realized he had gone off the road that night."

Emily sat quietly listening as Chester told his story. With tears streaming down her face she watched as the old man twisted the truth, the only way he was able to live with himself. Just as he had described to Theo the death of his parents, he justified his actions and claimed Chase's death to be an unfortunate accident. But it wasn't an accident and neither was the death of Theo's parents. They were the actions of a sick man, a man who had spent years living out the fantasies of a young man who lived vicariously through the adventures he read about in pirate novels and children's books.

A sickening feeling came over her as she watched his expression change from one of reflection to one of cold calculation and she realized he was planning her demise. Frantically searching around her for a way to escape the persistent barking of a dog drew her attention as well as Chester's.

"Damn it!" He grunted, heading for the basement stairs. Turning back to face Emily he raised the shotgun, "Don't even think about moving." He instructed before disappearing up the stairs.

While Emily listened, she heard a loud bang followed by two gunshots and then silence. As she held her breath anticipating the worst she heard someone call out her name.

"Emily! Emily are you here?" A man's voice rang out from upstairs.

"I'm down here!" She shouted in response.

The footsteps of several people could be heard coming toward her directions and she continued to direct them to her location. She was relieved to see three armed police officers run down the basement stairs to her.

"You're okay." One officer announced, "We got him."

Chapter 44

When the police had arrived at Chester's estate they had broken down the front door and had been greeted by Chester pointing a shotgun in their faces. The insistent barking of the neighbor's dog, who had been unfortunate enough to jump on Chester when he returned to the property and had been brutally kicked, his leg broken; had alerted the police to the area. Seeing the car they had been searching for in the driveway, they realized they had found their man and were discussing their plan of action when the dog alerted Chester to their presence.

Once Chester had been shot and killed and Emily had been found, they had informed Philip and Theo who rushed to the hospital to be by her side. After an extensive search of the property in Newport as well as the lake house, the police were able to piece together Chester's plan. A rental car had been found in the garage of the estate and the lake house was stocked with enough supplies to last him a year.

The police believed that he hadn't originally intended to kidnap Emily, but seeing how she reacted to his appearance at the shop had sent him over the edge. It looked as though he had spent a few days at the empty estate which allowed him time to drop off the journal, rent a car and prepare to leave his old life behind. After he kidnapped Emily, they believed he panicked and had held up there, hoping no one would find him while he figured out what to do with her.

Calls to St. Lucia had confirmed that though he had spent nearly two months there, he had returned to the area and had been traveling back and forth between the lake house and the cottage, keeping a watchful eye on both Philip and Emily. When he had seen them meet up with Theo they figured he knew it was only a matter of time before they knew everything and so he had tried to plant doubt in Emily's mind by giving her the journal. Having no way of knowing that Philip had already revealed so much, he was most likely shocked by her reaction to his sudden appearance.

Although the police initially suspected his attorney might be involved in some way, they were able to clear him of any involvement and his cooperation with the investigation ultimately led them to discover several assets that Chester had hidden, perhaps to live off for the remainder of his life.

Nearly a year after the case was closed; Emily received a substantial inheritance from Chester's estate, which she used to establish a scholarship in Chase's name at Brown University. Though Philip had not yet signed the paperwork officially buying out the company, Chester's attorney had been instructed by him to prepare the paperwork and so he was now the proud owner of Excursion Charters. Surprisingly but perhaps due to earlier guilt, Chester had left a sizable inheritance to Philip as well and he used it to pay off the business debts and to purchase the property adjacent to Emily's on the cove.

Chapter 45

Emily smiled as she watched Vicky and Aiden play with their little girl Amanda on the shore while Cara strolled hand in hand with her latest boyfriend along the beach. It was an open invitation to the little cove and one that her friends delighted in accepting at least a couple times a month. Aiden was in charge of the beer and Vicky and Cara were responsible for dessert while Emily and Philip provided the rest.

It had been nearly three years since Chester had been shot and killed by the local police after kidnapping Emily and holding her in the basement of his empty estate and yet the wounds were still healing. Afraid to live alone after the event, Philip had insisted she move into his condo until they were able to complete work on the new cottage, which was located next door to her own. They delighted in each other's company and continued their efforts in treasure hunting, though little else had been found. Still though they fantasized about finding a treasure chest filled with coins and jewels and imagined what they would do with their fortune, even though neither one of them could imagine a better life than they had now.

While Philip continued to run Excursion Charters and Emily ran her little book shop, Theo had disappeared as quickly as he had come into their lives. He would occasionally send them a postcard from some far off location, he had left Rhode Island and all the painful memories behind.

Philip was forever introducing Emily to single men in his employ, but even so, she had refused to date seriously and so, while she enjoyed the occasional dinner out, she preferred the single life. Occasionally

Philip remarked on the similarities between her and Sarah and that perhaps it was those traits that had attracted Chase to her.

Now as she sat amongst the most important people in her life, she smiled…content with her past and the years she had with Chase, the present she was now enjoying and the many adventures to come. As they raised their glasses to toast friendship, love and many more happy occasions Amanda ran toward them and shouted…

"Mommy…Daddy, look what I found!"

Also by Cheryl Kennedy:

The Forgotten Treaty

Prologue

1763

The thorny brush sliced into Nanatasis' legs as she ran through the forest. How long had it been since she had last heard the shouts of Wobi Sanoba the White Man who tracked her through these dense woods? Her lungs burned as she leapt over rocks and swift running brooks, tripping often as she repeatedly turned her head in search of her predator. Nanatasis' swollen belly tightened, protesting the unwelcome rush of adrenaline as she made one final attempt to put distance between herself and the Wobi Sanoba. She had lost track of time, unsure as to how long she had been running, though the distance between her and the village could not have been far. The cries of her people still echoed in her mind, pushing her ever onward. How many had been lost? She couldn't think about it now, she must focus her energy. The entrance to a familiar cave came into view.

Perhaps she could hide there until the sun went down and then backtrack to her village and her people.

Stopping at last to catch her breath, Nanatasis sat on a cool rock and stroked her belly. "Gawi", "Go to sleep" she whispered to the restless unborn child, "Oligawi", "Sleep well". Taking another deep breath, Nanatasis slowly rose only to feel the gush of her water breaking and the sharp pain of her first contractions. "Nda" –

"No" she screamed, forgetting for a moment that she was being hunted. Panic surged inside her as she spun around, searching the thick forest for signs of movement. The rustling of leaves followed by the sound of heavy footsteps trampling the earth as well as the frightened sounds of the wildlife brought the unwelcome realization. It was too late, as she feared; her scream was just what the Wobi Sanoba needed to pinpoint her location and he quickly pounced upon her. Nanatasis struggled to free herself, desperately pleading with her attacker, though she knew he couldn't understand her, not that it would have mattered. He didn't care that she was with child or that she was the Chief's daughter, he would take what he came for, regardless. Flailing her fists, she pounded the white man's chest as he held her by her arms, her feet dangling mere inches from the ground, kicking wildly to no avail. "Stop!" he commanded, "This will go much quicker if you cooperate." Nanatasis cried out as another contraction tore through her belly, stopping her momentarily from her struggles long enough for the man to regain control of his victim and toss her to the ground. Before she could catch the breath he had knocked out of her, the man tore her dress from her heaving body and pinned her shaking legs with his own. Grabbing her wrists he forced them above her head holding them there with one strong hand while he fondled her breasts with the other. The last thing Nanatasis saw as she gratefully blacked out was the Wobi Sanoba unfastening his trousers.

Kzowadowinno paced back and forth in his daughter's wigwam awaiting word from the tribesmen who were out searching for her. The white men had come unexpectedly. Though the battle was coming to an end, there were those who were not yet ready to lay down their weapons and surrender to the new laws. The result had been disastrous to both sides. For his own

Abenaki people it had meant the loss of many lives and the rape of many of the tribe's women. He prayed to the Gici Niwaskw The Great Spirit that this was not the case for Nanatasis, for she was not only with child, but was also his only daughter. A great celebration had been planned and the Gici Niwaskw had blessed his people with a bountiful harvest in honor of the first grandchild's approaching birth.

As Kzowadowinno continued to pace, the beat of the war drums in sync with the beating of his heart, his thoughts drifted to earlier memories. Images of Nanatasis taking her first steps, hugging her beloved Mateguas while he squirmed to escape, playing Wolf with the other children of the tribe, all the while seeking the love and affection of her father. Lost in his reverie Kzowadowinno did not hear the approach of the tribesmen as they entered the wigwam carrying the broken body of his daughter. Lying Nanatasis down on her bed of skins the warriors rose, standing in silence for Kzowadowinno to acknowledge their presence. Several minutes passed before the Chief turned, collecting himself. His eyes passed between the men and his daughter, trying to read their somber expressions. Nanatasis was alive; this was clear by her restless movements and subtle sobs. Kzowadowinno moved forward, closing the void between himself and his daughter. Though she was now clothed, her dress was torn and stained with blood, her lips swollen and bloody from where she had apparently bitten through the skin. Dried blood stained the length of her legs ending in the now soaked heels of her moccasins. Kzowadowinno's eyes scanned his daughter thoroughly before he rested his palm on her now empty belly.

The pain of the loss now evident on the tear streaked face of his daughter, she lifted her hand to lay it on top of her father's, her eyes remaining closed, shutting out the pain she would surely see in his own. A soft sob escaped her lips as the memories of her ordeal came rushing back. Her whole body ached, from the back of her head where it had slammed to the ground during her struggles with the Wobi Sanoba to the pain between her legs where she was brutally raped before she bore the child that the cruel man had hung by its own umbilical cord from a nearby birch limb before the warriors had arrived to rescue her. As the tears flowed from the corners of her eyes soaking her braids and pooling within the curves of her ears Kzowadowinno raised her in his arms, rocking her as he had when she was a child, singing to her as he stroked her hair until she fell into a deep slumber.

"Olegwasi." "Dream well." he whispered as he lowered her back down to her skins, covering her before kissing her forehead. As he rose, the warriors who had stood silent out of respect for their leader moved forward to await instruction. "Gao" "She sleeps" he stated, "Alsoda" "Let's go".

The warriors followed Kzowadowinno out of the wigwam, stepping aside as he stopped and looked back at his daughter one last time before bending to exit the shelter. Again he fell into silence, moving in the direction of the long house while the men followed behind.

Kzowadowinno sat in silence as the men described what they had seen. After leaving the village, the Wobi Sanoba had crossed through the meadow into the dense forest leaving broken limbs and muddy footprints. It had been easy enough to pursue him as his desire to capture Nanatasis greatly outweighed his wish to deceive his trackers. He didn't need to outsmart the natives, just outrun them, leaving enough distance between himself and the warriors to give him time to overpower the Chief's daughter. It had nothing to do with her beauty; it was about her status in the tribe. Once he had taken her she would bring shame upon her people, the father of her child would be forced to turn his back on her and her father would be disgraced. After her father stepped aside as Chief it would be easy to influence the new leader to sign over the lands and the tribe would be forced to retreat back to their original home in the White Mountains or better yet, to the Northern Territory.

Over the past decade the tribe had been spreading out, but the time had come to drive them north and claim the territory, which was prime for, not only fishing and hunting, but farming as well. The tribe had felt the pressure of these white men before as they occasionally torched their homes and shot at their hunters but this time it was different, more planned out and the losses had been far greater, both to their people and to their properties.

The warriors described in detail what they saw, unable to look at their Chief, knowing the pain their words would bring him. They had arrived just as the Wobi Sanoba was disappearing into the vast forest on foot. Two of the warriors followed in pursuit while the remaining pair stayed behind. Awasos, the leader of the warriors; as his strength was that of the great bear for which he was named; knelt to attend to Nanatasis while Pziko, the second in command focused on the deceased child, removing him from the limb and wrapping him in preparation for burial.

Awasos lowered his head as he related how he redressed Nanatasis and carried her back to the village and her people. Kzowadowinno, distraught with shame and disappointment at his grandson's loss instructed Awasos to gather the Grand Council in the council house at sunset where they would discuss the day's events and come to a decision regarding what repercussions were to be invoked on the Wobi Sanoba. "Alosa." "Go." Kzowadowinno instructed, rising before the warriors, indicating the end of the conversation. It was time he go to the sweat lodge and consult with Gici Niwaskw.

As the Civil Chief, Kzowadowinno often relied on The Great Spirit as an instrumental guide to the spirit world. It was The Great Spirit who aided the Chief in his most important decisions involving his tribe. Kzowadowinno settled in, smoking from the pipe and allowing his mind and body to soar with the eagles in search of the answers he sought. As the hours passed unnoticed, Kzowadowinno's spirit rose above his earthly body, visiting each of his options and weighing them heavily before moving to the next; each stop filled with images of his grieving daughter and her empty belly. When finally he stepped outside of the lodge, moving in the direction of the council house, the Chief had made his decision, the only choice he could have made.

Facing the Chief sat the members of the Grand Council, those remaining after the devastating battle of the day. Kzowadowinno nodded his greetings to the tribe, they in turn bowing their heads to his presence. Several minutes passed in silence before Kzowadowinno addressed the tribe, who patiently awaited his instruction. In the soft-spoken words of a broken man, the Chief acknowledged the tragedies of the day. The losses had been many, amongst who was the War Chief, who had held the position for nearly two decades. As the only remaining Chief of the tribe, it fell upon Kzowadowinno to not only instruct his people on their peaceful path, but also regarding whatever vengeance may lie ahead for the Wobi Sanoba who had shamed both himself and his daughter.

The tribe sat still, listening intently as the Chief instructed several women to arrange for the earth burial of his grandson. He requested that the Medicine Man of the tribe tend to his ailing daughter while directing others to assist in the tracking of the Wobi Sanoba. As his final directive Kzowadowinno asked of The Great

Spirit that his tribe be watched over and be blessed with a swift end to this tragic circumstance.

Kzowadowinno led the tribe out of the council house, standing off to the side of the structure as each member departed to their various tasks. Taking the hands of the warriors who would begin their trek immediately, he whispered his blessings upon them, again asking The Great Spirit to watch over his men and bring them home safely.

As the days passed, Nanatasis grew weaker. Though her body had healed from her horrible ordeal, her mind had grown feeble and she suffered from delusions from which, not even the Medicine Man, could rescue her. Her cries and screams frightened the other women of the tribe such that they refused to enter her wigwam for fear that the evil spirits might infect them as well. Kzowadowinno spent countless hours praying to The Great Spirit for guidance, but no peace would come.

Finally on the tenth day, the warriors returned to the village, dragging the white man behind them. His face covered in blood and bruises, he struggled against his rawhide shackles, fearing his punishment would be far worse than anything he had inflicted upon their people, including the Chief's daughter. Hearing the ruckus, Kzowadowinno stepped from the sweat lodge, stopping short, "Awani na?" "Who is that?" he asked, knowing full well this was the evil man they sought and stepping closer to inspect the stranger before him.

Awasos stepped forward, bowing his head in greetings to his Chief. "Wobi Sanoba" he responded. Kzowadowinno circled around the white man as he in turn twisted his head to keep a keen eye on the Chief.

"Let me go before the others come back and finish what we started." The Wobi Sanoba screamed at his captors.

Without acknowledging the white man, the Chief gave orders to the warriors to tie him to a post on the far side of the village common.

As the warriors did as instructed, the remaining members of the tribe, with the exception of Nanatasis; who remained in her wigwam, gathered around the post chanting thanks to Gici Niwaskw for delivering the white man back to their village so that they might seek revenge for his evil deeds.

Kzowadowinno raised his arms, requesting silence from his people. As the tribe slowly calmed the Chief asked that they recall their peaceful nature and remember that the spirit of his grandson would live on forever. He spoke of their ancestors who had walked these grounds before them and to their descendants yet to breath life. The tribe listened quietly as he talked of the gifts that The Great Spirit had given them, the bountiful harvests and the plentiful game within these forests. It was obvious that Gici Niwaskw thought kindly of their gentle ways and had rewarded them with his offerings. Were they to turn their backs on these ways now simply because this evil white man had shamed his family, because their people had been slain during a battle that had gone on far too long already? The tribe members whispered amongst themselves in disbelief. How could their leader be so merciful when he had lost so much, when they had lost so much?

Again Kzowadowinno raised his arms to silence both their voices and their fears. It was true that the Wobi Sanoba did not deserve to live; it was also true that taking his life would be the easiest and quickest way to rid the village of the evil he possessed. Yet, despite all that had transpired, would it not be a more fitting punishment to invoke a treaty with this white man? Though unsure in their acceptance, the tribe nodded their agreement to their leader, bowing their heads again in shame for their unholy thoughts towards the white man.

At their agreement the Chief asked that the elder tribesmen join him in the sweat lodge where they could better contact The Great Spirit whose wisdom and vision they could channel in order to make a sound and just pact with the Wobi Sanoba. While one elder thought that The Great Spirit would be understanding of a swift and lethal end to the man, another felt any act upon him would bring draught and starvation to the village. At one point another elder considered an "eye for an eye" approach while the next voiced a proposal to abandon him to the beasts of the forest. In the end it was Kzowadowinno himself who saw what Gici Niwaskw wanted his people to do.

Kzowadowinno sent for a translator so that there would be no misunderstanding between his people and the Wobi Sanoba. While he patiently waited for the interpreter's arrival, Kzowadowinno prepared himself. Though already wearing a breechcloth topped by a band of bark fashioned as a belt, Kzowadowinno dressed in leggings made of deerskins, which were worn below the cloth. Normally such leggings were only worn during the winter months, however traditional ceremonial costume included both the leggings as well as a headdress. The headdress was constructed of feathers, porcupine quills and hair as well as animal skin and foxtails. On his feet the Chief wore traditional moccasins laced with rawhide ties and adorned with small shells.

Stepping from his wigwam, Kzowadowinno looked around him at what lingered of his village. Charred remains of what once was were scattered across the inner circle of the village, a reminder of what had been lost and what still needed to be done. A small group of women sat together under the shade of a maple tree, fastening beads and shells to a deerskin that would be wrapped around the Chief's shoulders for the day's important meeting. The women swayed in rhythm as they chanted prayers to The Great Spirit. To the right of the women stood a gathering of warriors, sharpening their arrowheads while talking amongst themselves, occasionally nodding in the direction of the white man, still fastened to the post. Kzowadowinno sighed heavily knowing that today would be a turning point for his people and it was up to him to lead them in the right direction, to ease their heartache and mend their wounds, somehow putting them on a path of forgiveness.

Entering his daughter's wigwam he stood just inside the structure while he took a deep breath in preparation of what was to come. The heartache she bore deepened by the loss of her husband mere days after her child from wounds suffered during the battle. It was probably for the best, for had he survived he would have been expected to turn his back on her for the shame she had caused him. Though her external wounds were now healed she had not spoken since her ordeal and Kzowadowinno feared he had also lost her. Her once rounded cheeks were now a hollow shell of what they once were and the circles under her eyes brought darkness to her normally bright laughing eyes. As he approached her bed of skins where she lay, Nanatasis visibly stiffened, her arms, which had lain limp at her sides now tensed as she squeezed her hands into fists. Her eyes were fixed on the roof of the wigwam, refusing to acknowledge his presence before her. Kzowadowinno wanted to reach out his hand to stroke her hair as he had so often when she was a child. The power of a father's love had been all she needed back then and time and time again he had soothed her scrapped knees and bruised ego with his palm on her back or a pat on the head. His very touch healing her every woe. Oh, but if it would be enough now. Instead he stood before her unable to sooth her pain. No spoken words could comfort her fragile state of mind, which was quickly retreating to a place far too distant for even her father to reach.

Stepping inside the wigwam and pulling him from his reflections, Awasos informed the Chief that the interpreter had arrived and the Grand Council was awaiting his presence. Nodding in acknowledgement, Kzowadowinno glanced again at his daughter before exiting her dwelling in route to the council house. Upon entering, Kzowadowinno greeted his tribe as well as the man Jeremiah who had translated for his people on more than one occasion. Jeremiah respected the peaceful ways of the Abenaki people who had raised him as one of their own when his own family had been executed by their fellow settlers for views regarding the natives that were not in keeping with the directive of the new government. After the execution, the settlers had simply abandoned Jeremiah who was not yet eight seasons old. Kzowadowinno had taken him under his wing, having no sons of his own and raised him in the ways of his people. The Chief taught him how to fish and hunt as well as plant seeds so that one day he could provide for his own family. When Jeremiah grew into a man, Kzowadowinno had insisted that he leave the village and dwell amongst his own kind. As difficult as it had been to go, Jeremiah understood that his place was with the white man and not with the natives, though time and time again he had returned to the village to act as a translator on important issues between the two.

Now Kzowadowinno had requested his assistance regarding a much more personal matter and Jeremiah was greatly honored to be in attendance. Kzowadowinno commenced the meeting with a prayer to Gici Niwaskw. The Chief asked that The Great Spirit bless his people with the ability to forgive the Wobi Sanoba for his transgressions while enacting a just punishment. The white man knelt at the feet of Awosos and Pziko who held him down with a hand upon each of his shoulders preventing him from rising. Jeremiah translated to the man, the words of the treaty as spoken by Kzowadowinno, while writing them on parchment to be signed by all parties if agreeable. The treaty stated that in order to put an end to the fighting, the Abenaki people agreed to surrender their lands to the settlers. In doing so, the Wobi Sanoba would permit their people safe travel to the north without the fear of attack. The treaty also stated that upon surrender of these sacred lands, on which many of his tribe as well as his only grandchild had been buried, the man must sacrifice the first born child of his first born. Once agreed upon, this treaty would remain in effect as long as the he and his descendents laid claim to the land. Thus, the punishment would be carried down from generation to generation.

Having knelt in silence through the reading of the treaty, the white man was now given the opportunity to speak, should he choose to do so. Jeremiah, having explained the treaty now added that it would be in his best interest to agree to the tribe's terms as his refusal would surely bring far greater consequences. Jeremiah held out the quill to the man, "They have two days to leave this land." he spat, signing the parchment and knocking the warriors hands from his shoulders. Looking around at the angry faces of the natives before settling his eyes on the Chief, the man rose and added, "Your people have soiled this land long enough, and it is time you take your leave. My kind greatly outnumber your own but for the sake of those who have seen to many lose their lives in this battle, I will grant you the terms you have asked. Understand that I will allow the safe passage of your people to the north, but as to sacrifices let it be known that your Gici Niwaskw does not hold court over my people. My God alone will decide what sacrifices, if any, will befall me or my descendents." With that, the man exited the council house, never to be seen by the tribe again.

****

Chapter 1

The takeover couldn't have come at a more inopportune time. Though she was confident that her standing as Executive Director was secure, Lily knew that the announcement of her unexpected pregnancy had caused more than a few raised eyebrows and she had to wonder if it could put her in a vulnerable position. That being said, now was not the time to start second-guessing her decision to disclose that information, not with her biggest event of the year only three months away. Besides, she was only a couple months into her first trimester; she had plenty of time to impress the new management before she had to take her leave.

Stepping out of the shower Lily felt the now all too familiar wave of nausea and she rushed to the toilet without stopping to grab a towel. Dry heaves were the worst, the bile of an empty stomach rising to her throat, burning her insides as she spewed out whatever liquids remained in her belly from the night before. This had been going on for more than a month now, yet knowing it would come didn't change the fact that she simply couldn't get any food in her before ten o'clock. Just the thought of food in the morning was enough to make her turn green. Flushing the toilet, Lily reached for a nearby towel and looked at her reflection in the mirror. Wiping her damp hair away from her face she frowned at the pale reflection of her image in front of her. Her once shiny brown hair now looked drab and limp, her normally olive complexion now pale and blotchy. Ugh, Lily thought as she wiped the steam building on the mirror, I look exactly how I feel, like crap. Picking up her toothbrush and toothpaste, Lily took a deep, steadying breath in preparation of the taste that would either settle or upset her delicate stomach. Over the past couple of weeks, scents and tastes that normally would have been appealing to her now sent her running to the nearest bathroom. Lily hadn't been able to keep the pregnancy a secret from her coworkers once the morning sickness came.

Available at better book stores or online at
www.a-argusbooks.com